Vivia

Midwestern ✷ Midcentury ✷ Memories

BJ CLARK

*Dear Ann —
I am so happy to know such a beautiful, wonderful woman! Have fun!*

BJ

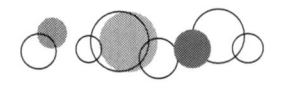

VIVID • Midwestern • Midcentury • Memories
©2019 BJ Clark
All rights reserved.

No part of this book may be reproduced or transmitted in any form or by any means, electronic or mechanical, including photocopying, recording or by any information storage and retrieval system, without written permission from the author. You may not reprint, resell or distribute the contents of this book without express written permission from the author.

All violations will be remedied with legal action and justice will be sought to the maximum penalty allowable by law in the State in which the original purchaser resides.

Managing Editor and Alchemist: Robin Shukle
Design & Production: Liz Mrofka, What If? Publishing
Cover Art: Ryan Armour
Printed by: CreateSpace

BJ Clark
Loveland, CO

ISBN-13: 9781798229361

Table of Contents

Dedication 4
Preface—Moving 5
The Umbrella. 13
An Allotment of Chicken Hawks 21
Gravy. 27
The Dining Room 34
The First Time I Saw Paris (poem). 47
The Blue Hole 49
Rosie 55
The Last House in the Neighborhood. 63
The Little Black Bag. 69
Spring 77
Coffee 87
Halloween 1953 95
There Goes the Neighborhood 103
The Christmas Pageant 113
The Gambler 119
Honeysuckle 129
Going Home 133
The Lamp 145
Mink 151
Wouldn't You Really Rather Drive A Buick 161
Afterword. 167
With Gratitude. 171

Dedication

For Roger and Tim,
my husband and my brother,
the two men who have always supported me
in the pursuit of happiness.

Preface ✸ Moving

Dad and me.
Moving on.

1950: October: A perfect fall day: West Bend, Wisconsin.

On what seemed like any other day, my father threw two huge automotive vacuum cleaners in his car and drove off to create a new future for our family. As my mother, brother, and I stood in the driveway, waving after him, my mother was the only person who had any idea of what was going on.

Apparently, my father had been frustrated, "cooped up," he said, in his office at The West Bend Aluminum company. There had been no sign of his displeasure, but he said it had been coming on for some time.

Our family lived in a small brick house on a tree-lined street in West Bend, Wisconsin. There were just a few houses on the block, mostly like ours, small brick bungalows. I had started kindergarten, and on the very first day, I got lost on the way home. As far as I can tell, that was the one exciting moment I remember about being in West Bend; otherwise, my West Bend memories are pretty much those that people told me.

I do know my parents had friends, got a brand-new car, and played bridge with couples that my father knew through his work at the West Bend Aluminum Company.

He had a good job as the general sales manager for what became a big company in the world of cookware and small appliances. Dad said he liked the people in West Bend. He said they were friendly and optimistic, but he also admitted that he just couldn't stand his job. He'd been a traveling salesman for years when he met and married my mother, but in deference to being able to spend more time with the family, he took a desk job to try and teach other salesmen the tricks he'd learned after years on the road. He had some good stories, but most of the photos I saw of Dad in his early years were largely serious, featuring him talking on the phone, probably to some guy on the road with a problem, or worse yet, poor sales.

He told mother that he could have fixed the guy's problem in minute if he'd been there, if he hadn't been tied to a big desk in an office building. He itched to be back on the road, but mother preferred West Bend, which was also close to family relatives.

Mom said that one day Dad came home all excited. He pulled into the driveway and pulled a huge vacuum cleaner out of its backseat.

"Come here, Dena! Hurry! You won't believe my great news."

Mother said she did hurry, especially because she knew that West Bend Aluminum did not sell any vacuum cleaners. When she got to the car and looked at Dad's face as he dusted off the vacuum cleaner with his pocket handkerchief, she knew that changes were about to be discussed.

He started to talk even faster than he usually did. "You won't believe this, but Oscar Shotlander took me out to lunch today and told me about a new kind of sales job. It's called a manufacturer's rep, where the salesman just represents a company to sell their product; they don't employ him. He makes a percentage of the sales and keeps track of his own time. Generally, he decides who to sell to and how to sell in a territory he's given. Then, and this is what I couldn't believe, he said I could have a territory—in this case, Ohio, if I wanted to sell these Huntington Car Vacuums to car dealers and others who professionally clean up cars for resale or as a part of their customer service.

"I know this is a new trend because he told me about it before, but today he told me the sales figures, and when I figure what I can make in a big automotive state like Ohio, I could leave West Bend tomorrow, knowing I'd make more than I make now in a matter of months. I know it's risky, but I just know I could make this work. Besides, as a manufacturer's rep, I can represent other automotive products and sell several things to each prospect. I've just never seen anything like this job before. I'm sure I can be successful and I'll be my own boss. I won't have to stay on the road for weeks at a time. I probably could travel from Monday to Friday by working the territory on that schedule."

My mother said, "Bob, take a breath." That became a favorite phrase of hers in later years, but this might have been the first time she used it. "I know you're excited, and this may be a good thing. If you're really that unhappy at West Bend, you probably do need to leave. I always have and will support you, but let's go inside to do some figuring."

When they finished figuring, things must have looked good because my father gave notice to West Bend within two weeks, telling everyone he was going to miss them, wouldn't be competing with their products, and just needed to be a real salesman again. "It's what I know. It's who I am, and I really am good at it."

No one questioned that part. West Bend quickly arranged

a good-bye party and gave him some new golf clubs to remember them by. He always said the guys from West Bend were great, and he kept a picture of his weekly golf foursome on his wall in his home office until he died—more than fifty years later. For me, it meant the end of kindergarten; I didn't mind.

Dad's dream took us to Northern Ohio, near Lake Erie, to a little town of about 11,000 people. He said it looked like New England. He liked the people, and he had a good account in town who offered to help him find a nice house.

That's how my parents began a new kind of journey, one they took along with many other young modern people home from the war, who left the community of their first-generation immigrant parents, siblings, and relatives, to settle in places that offered new opportunities far from home.

Dad took advantage of a modern trend where "developers" created neighborhoods and communities to suit the optimism of the post-war generation, to help them realize their dreams of having their own home, even if it meant living in neighborhoods filled with people who were not like them. Our new neighborhood was Dutch, Canadian, Italian, English, German, and Irish, mixed together. All had found the means to purchase a new home from among those that were being built. The religious cultures of the neighbors—Catholic, Protestant, Jewish, and even Mormon—mixed and melded, usually without slurs or enmity, because they knew each other, lived near or next door to one another.

As we moved into our new house, we greeted our

neighbors eagerly, knowing that since we were far from home, away from the roots that our family had planted in this country, we would have to find friends, most likely neighbors, who would bond with us and become like family to us. As others also moved in as part of this new American Dream, the dream of becoming a land (home) owner, they viewed their experience as moving forward to achieve the immigrant dreams of their parents.

The rest of the story of how this worked out is included in the following pages. They reflect the memories I have of my childhood, in this newly minted neighborhood, along with the stories I heard from my parents and those of the neighbors who became our dear friends.

Now, the dreams of home ownership, moving for a career, and the opportunities my father aspired to are everyday occurrences, but then they meant major changes. These times reflect people not only moving once, but several times. Neighborhoods are not as closely knit; now neighborly contact involves places to visit on the front lawn or to share a key in case of emergencies. People work; they don't spend as much time in their houses. Their children have various types of childcare not necessarily related to their home. The neighborhood that we knew as children is becoming deconstructed to the point that many people don't know all the names of people on their block. While people are friendly, they are often not connected by sharing life stories or extensive social time.

What you read here may be a reminiscence of an earlier time, but it is as true as memory ever is and reflects the spirit of the people involved. Certainly, names have been changed to ensure that no one gets recognized for things they may or may not have done. However, I can say, without reservation, that I live with admiration and affection for all of those who made such a positive, and mostly loving, contribution to my life. My memories do reflect, largely, the trust and deep friendship that we shared. Not a bad start for a girl whose favorite memories involve the love, laughter, and optimism of that special time.

The Umbrella

Our porch with the umbrella.

* ✲ *

As a child of the Fifties, I grew up in a ranch-style house, long, low, sided with a mixture of clapboard and indiscriminate stone. The house's most notable design feature was the waist-high stone wall that ran the length of the front of house, ending in a high lamppost.

Entry to the house required using a side walkway to skirt both the wall and the lamppost. I'm certain that this design was intended to set our house apart from the other no-wall, no-lamppost houses in the neighborhood, but I usually thought of it as creating a perfect place for Dad's umbrella on the inside of the wall.

Shortly after we moved in and planted two pencil-thin trees in front of the wall for shade, my father announced that the wide concrete expanse between the wall and the house would serve as a perfect place for entertaining. With that end in mind, he assembled a giant white wrought-iron table and stuck an equally big black-and-white umbrella in the hole in its center. He added an assortment of chairs to surround the table and then proceeded to line up three other smaller chair and cocktail table sets to provide additional options for snacking and neighborhood viewing.

"It's almost like a real front porch," he told my mother. "Only the umbrella will make it even better."

"You mean it will be almost like a patio," my mother replied.

"No," my father said. "This will be our front porch. A patio is usually toward the back or side of the house. Patios are for people you invite to your house, but a porch involves all the people you see in the neighborhood. People can drop in without a special invitation."

He went on, but I didn't listen, thinking they were simply having arguments about the faux distinctions of the Fifties. I, on the other hand, was much more interested in important things. When would I be as tall as the lamppost? Could I hide behind the wall, hurl a water balloon at someone on the street and get back down, moving quickly enough to go unnoticed? I asked myself big questions to avoid thinking about porches, patios, and the embarrassment of seeing my father unfurl the giant umbrella as he started hollering at the neighbors.

"Look here, Sam. I've got a new umbrella. We're all set for cocktails. Come on over and we'll try out this new set up."

Mr. Rizzo, our neighbor from across the street, had been on his way to his mailbox, but he waved back at my father, immediately changed directions, and started crossing the street.

"Look here, Bill. Come on over and have a drink."

Bill Roley, from the house on the corner, waved too. He had been trimming the baby shrub in his front yard, but he quickly put down his clippers and joined Sam in crossing the street.

"How about you, Harry?" Dad hollered to Mr. Shadley, who lived right next door.

Mr. Shadley, who had a wheelbarrow full of plantings, waved and said, "No thanks, Bob. Got to get this done before the sun goes down."

My father smiled and said. "Gee, Harry, if you get all that stuff done, you'll just have to take care of it, and you'll never have time for a drink!"

Mr. Roley and Mr. Rizzo laughed, but Mr. Shadley went around the side of his house without another word.

As Mr. Roley and Mr. Rizzo took a seat, Dad poured them all a clear drink in glasses that looked like triangles from the side. There were olives, cocktail napkins, a few nuts, and the beginning of conversation.

"Well, if you ask me," Mr. Rizzo started, "Harry Shadley's not going to have fun when the sun goes down either."

All the men laughed, clinked their glasses and said, "Here's to good neighbors."

After deciding that I'd have to practice my balloon-hurling technique, estimating it would take six years to reach the full height of the lamp post, I went inside. My mother was getting things ready to begin fixing dinner, but she kept going to the kitchen window to listen in on what was happening under the umbrella.

"Your father," she said shaking her head. "I think he's really started something with that umbrella."

The years proved her right. For more than twenty years, on Friday afternoons long before TGIF, when my father returned home from his weekly travels, the umbrella went up, signaling the beginning of the weekend.

The kitchen window also played a lasting role in helping my brother and me learn things we did and did not want to know.

During one of the umbrella sessions, when Mr. Rizzo was the only guest, I learned that he'd been to jail. When Mr. Roley came by himself on another day, I learned how he got shot in the leg at Iwo Jima and had a nervous breakdown. It was the one and only time I heard these stories, and although I learned it was important to keep the secrets of your friends from my father's example, I felt guilty for knowing secrets I'd learned as an eavesdropper.

More often than not, the friends and conversations that were gathered under the umbrella were of the ordinary kind, sharing daily observations and joint confirmations of what's acceptable. However, there were the other times when I learned what my father meant when he explained the difference between a porch and a patio. There were days when guests came uninvited.

One day my little artery-hardened grandmother had taken her lemonade and newspaper out under the umbrella. It was a hot day, and as she fanned herself with the paper, she said "hello" to a young Bible-carrying couple who were walking in front of the house. Nana always said "hello" to people passing by, but in this case she obviously did not recognize these two as the Jehovah's Witnesses that they were.

Fortunately, I was at the kitchen window, getting a glass of water, and I did not move in anticipation of what was about to happen.

"Hello to you," the dour young man said. "Do you have a few minutes for us?" he asked as he approached the porch. She nodded as he proceeded with Bible-thumping statements about the "din of the world" and the "noise of Satan's angry voice." He continued, at length, as my grandmother nodded. "What do you think?" he finally asked. "Do you see my point?"

"No," she responded sweetly. "You must have some other place in mind. This is really quite a quiet neighborhood, but it's been nice to visit with you."

The man and woman looked at each other, stunned, momentarily mute. "Yes, yes," he finally said softly. "Well, I guess we'll be going. We'll just leave these materials right here." They quickly left the porch and the neighborhood, making no other stops along the way.

"Well," Nana said when she came back into the house. "I met the nicest couple who stopped to chat. They'd had the most awful time!" She took her glass to the sink and placed her newspaper and the Witness materials on the table. "I think I'm done with all these," she said. "Some people really do have terrible stories to tell."

Other times, cars would pull over and people would ask directions of whoever was sitting on the porch. Men selling vacuum cleaners would offer to demonstrate how well their products could suck up the leaves that found their way under the umbrella. Kids would come to sell candy and newspapers over the wall. Oftentimes, the response to such encounters would come by way of the kitchen window.

However, most of the times and things I remember about the umbrella, the front porch and the kitchen window, were fun-filled, well intentioned, and joyful. While I learned how important it was to listen to friends and to keep their secrets, I also learned the importance and healing power of laughter. I learned that whenever it's possible, it's a good idea to choose to be happy.

Some people never learn that. Harry Shadley never did come over to our house. Instead, he chose to worry about noise, even on Friday nights. Eventually, Harry died three days after he retired, with everything done, everything tended, and all responsibilities met. (The new neighbors let Harry's lawn and planting go completely to pot.) He didn't have a funeral, my father observed. That would have been too much like a party for Harry, but my father did feel Harry's loss. He noted that Harry was the only complainer of the bunch. "He made the rest of us look tolerable," Dad said. "I'll be forever grateful."

I'm grateful for the memories especially of the times when Harry would holler, "Quiet down over there—you're keeping me up!" and my father would respond, "Well, Harry, if you don't like the noise come on over." Harry never came.

Toward the end of the umbrella era, Harry had had it one night and called the cops. The cops came, heard the stories about Harry, and stayed until it was time to clean up. There were no reports in the paper.

Now, as one who is older than my father was when he purchased his first umbrella, I have few regrets other than not living in a house with a porch and an umbrella like the one in my childhood, one that allowed the world to drop in on me.

An Allotment of Chicken Hawks

Hawk in pursuit.

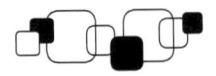

My father sought his fortune as a manufacturer's representative for automotive products in Ohio, in a small town near Lake Erie, one that had good schools, and U.S. Route 60 within two blocks of our house. My father could get in his car to drive to his sales calls in no time, and the rest of the family could reside in a neighborhood that was called an "allotment." This was before the words "developer" and "development" were coined, a time when parcels of land were cut and figured into lots for houses while remaining inside a stated "allotment" of land.

This kind of neighborhood was brand new, one in which all the neighbors were new, like us, with no history or ready gossip to share. It was a step up for many people, and the word "luxury" was used in the sales material. Although "luxury" didn't mean "fancy," it did mean the houses could stand up to a storm and were built for a lifetime of use.

Other places in the country were also developing neighborhoods this way. Some were known just by their names, as in Levittown, but our allotment was unusual in some ways, especially because it was designed to include different types of houses. A buyer could purchase a big house or a much smaller house, but the houses were mixed together, next to each other, all nice enough but some recognizably nicer than others.

After moving my mother from her childhood home in Wisconsin, my father bought her a house as big as his imagination would allow. It was first on the block, and even though it wouldn't seem big in later decades, it was large for its time. There were enough bedrooms for everyone, and enough baths too, hardwood floors, which my mother immediately covered with some nondescript carpet, central heating, a separate dining room, and bay windows. My mother and father were thrilled. However, after several months, they were most thrilled that the neighborhood still had few enough houses that my brother and I could play and wander around the allotment without worrying anyone.

It was only two blocks to a field where we could fly kites, and next to that a woods filled with birds, deer, and other mostly harmless wildlife. To my parents, it seemed like something they'd read about, in town but really not of town, almost like a small place in the country with neighbors.

It didn't take much time for us to create adventures. My little brother, who was four, followed me everywhere—into the fields, into the woods, lagging behind to pick things up, then running to catch up before I got out of sight. Still little, he often brought a small toy "friend" on his journey. Sometimes, he took a stuffed bear or bunny, but most often a little squeaky rubber mouse that he'd gotten on Halloween. He loved the mouse because I hated it, a rotten rubber smelly thing with stiff black whiskers, and a blood-red mouth sporting a dark red spot dripping from its lower lip.

"It's so funny," he would say. "Look here, BJ." He'd stick the mouse into my face, show his teeth and let out some kind of silly squeal. It drove me crazy. When he followed me down the block carrying his little rubber vermin, I'd walk faster to get ahead. It worked fine for me, but he kept yelling.

"Wait up," he'd plead. "I won't show you the mouse. Pleeeeeze wait."

He should have thought of that earlier, I thought to myself. I scurried on until I was a block's length ahead of him when he crossed the staked land line at the end of the block.

The field had been mowed. There were crows circling overhead, and the sky was getting gray. We'd have to go home soon, with the rain coming, but I wanted to teach my brother a lesson.

"Come here," I hollered. "Come all the way into the field. Come see what I've found."

"What is it?"

" You'll have to come and see. Leave your mouse there."

"No. I'll lose him." He came running toward me, holding his ugly mouse aloft.

Thunder rumbled, and he ran faster, still holding his mouse high above his head.

"This is scary," he cried, just as a large shadow formed over his head. The shadow twirled in the sky, got bigger, got smaller, then swooped down in an instant. I saw it coming first and dropped to the ground, but he kept on running until he felt the edge of a talon touch his hand as it grabbed the rubber mouse and flew skyward.

My brother screamed as I looked up to see the hawk make a turn away from us and gain altitude. It was a huge bird, with wide wings and long legs that ended in the clawed feet that held my brother's rubber mouse in their grip.

"Wow," I said as I ran over to him. "I was afraid he was going to grab you!"

"No, no, no," he cried, "but he got mousy. "

I feigned no sympathy. "Fine with me, I replied."

I looked up and saw the hawk flying off. He was getting smaller, not as scary, but his shrill cry filled miles of air.

"That scared me," my brother said, looking down at the ground, carefully looking at the ground ahead of him. He took a step toward me. "I'm not coming here with you anymore."

"Fine with me," I repeated.

"Oh no, look!" He pointed toward something on the ground.

There was mousy, his stomach torn open, one eye just a hole with rubber edges. My brother leaned over for a closer inspection, then kicked his old friend deep into the woods.

"Mousy's done," he said. "That bird killed him, but he's not going to get me. What kind of bird was that?" he asked as he looked up.

"Perhaps a chicken hawk. They eat flesh. I heard Mr. Rizzo tell Dad there were chicken hawks around here."

He shook his head. "Poor mousy. Why did he want a mouse if he's a chicken hawk?"

"Some things are a mystery," I replied. "Like why little brothers want to ask stupid questions."

"You're not the big deal you think you are," he said. "And you never will be either. Next time I'm going to go into the woods. I don't think the hawks fly into the woods."

"No, there are only big snakes squirming around in there," I laughed.

My brother winced, but I wasn't sorry about mousy or excited about more adventures with my brother either.

We walked the rest of the way home in silence. I walked slowly: he kept up. Thankfully, it was almost time for dinner.

Gravy

Pass the gravy.

My father once told me that there were two types of women, those who made gravy and those who didn't. He explained that those women who made gravy were generous and caring women who would accommodate the wishes and desires of others. Those who did not were suspect. And far worse, the no-gravy ladies were likely to be self-centered, stingy, and definitely no fun.

He provided me with this revelation when I was ten years old, as we were driving in his beloved Buick Roadmaster along the back roads outside of Columbus, Ohio, on a particularly gray, rainy November day. We were going to the home of a cousin whom my father had been avoiding for years. "I'll bet she won't be making any gravy. She's that type," he said. "She'll work you around to where she wants you. She'll get you to come to her house, but then it'll all be over. There won't be any gravy."

I couldn't believe what I was hearing. Why were we choosing to drive such a long distance to have dinner in a place where we knew we wouldn't enjoy either the company or the food? Worse than that, why in this overheated, steamy car, where the defroster didn't work and where the radio was tuned only to sports channels, was he ranting about gravy? It didn't make sense, but that was nothing new.

"Don't forget what I've told you," he went on without missing a beat. "You definitely don't want to be one of those no-gravy women. Make sure your mother teaches you to make gravy. Better yet, get your Aunt Leona to teach you. She makes her gravy with cornstarch. The gravy has a special sheen; it shines in the bowl. Unbelievable. But we won't be getting gravy today, and if it's chicken, you can be sure she'll serve the necks and backs too. Your cousin got weaned on city life. If she could, she'd get everything ready-made at the store. If you become that kind of woman, you'll lead a lonely life."

"She won't be lonely," I whispered. "We're visiting her aren't we?" I was still puzzled by the gravy talk. My father could and did talk about anything, but this conversation created an entirely new dimension.

"What?" He paused. Then the words came in a rush. "We have to visit your cousin because we told your grandmother we would. It's as simple as that. Your mother and brother are out of town, and we have no excuse, except the truth, and that won't fly. You just can't tell your cousin that you don't want to visit her when your grandmother says you will. You can't say, 'You're miserable company and you can't cook.' It's just not that simple. You have to humor your grandmother or you'll set a whole bad cycle in motion. Your grandmother will tell your mother, there will be conversations about respect, about the family falling apart, and finally there won't be any more good dinners at home either. Everything will be disrupted. It won't be worth it, and that's why we're going. We'll stay two hours, say good things about the backs and necks of chickens, ducks, or whatever, then we'll go and be done with it."

"But what if I really don't like the food?" I asked. "I know I can move it around on my plate, but I'm not supposed to lie. What am I going to say?"

"Just say 'it's interesting,'" he answered. "That's what all smart people say when they don't know what to say. Interesting is in the mind of the beholder, so no one can say you are lying. Just say 'what an interesting flavor,' or if you really get stuck, you can always say 'I've never had anything quite like this before.' Believe me, that will be the truth."

With that, we lapsed into momentary silence, as we turned the corner and pulled up to the curb in front of my cousin's apartment building. I thought the building looked like a nice place. Trees lined the streets and the people who were walking their dogs nodded to us and smiled as we got out of the car.

My father opened the back car door and took a large Whitman's Sampler box from the back seat. "These chocolates will really please your grandmother," he said. "Your cousin's bound to mention that I brought the Whitman's and not the Fannie Farmer. Details make a difference."

He winked and we entered the apartment building. Our cousin, who was about my father's age, met us in the hall. I was introduced to her as Cousin Maggie, and even though I wondered if this familiar introduction indicated some form of disrespect, I greeted her with a firm "how do you do" and extended my hand.

When she shook my hand and said, "Well how do you do to you too," she smiled. I didn't think she looked the least bit self-centered, stingy, or no fun. She was wearing a soft pink fuzzy sweater, "angora" she called it, and a long gray skirt with flat black shoes. She had soft-looking shoulder-length brown hair and a nice complexion. She looked beautiful to me. She definitely didn't look at all like a lonely person.

"Why, Bob, this is quite a box of candy. Thank you! You're all quite civilized," she said, as she motioned for us to go inside.

As we entered her apartment, we were in the middle of a long hallway. Family photos and pictures of friends covered both walls. At the very end of the hallway, on the lower right-hand side, she'd even made room for a picture of our family. My mother was holding my baby brother, and I was standing beside my father, holding his hand.

"I hope you don't mind," she said, "but I think we'll eat right away. I'm trying something new, and I don't know how I'm doing on my timing." We passed through the living room quickly and moved right into the dining room.

My father winked as she headed for the kitchen. She turned around. "Seat yourselves," she said, and motioned to either side of the table. It had been set for three, and it had been set with a fancy tablecloth that had silver threads running through it. The napkins matched, there were shiny silver knives, forks, and spoons, and the dishes had pink flowers all around the edges. The whole setup looked like something I'd seen in the movies. I could almost see a guy dressed in a tuxedo coming from the kitchen. Unlike our house, there weren't any little jars or bottles of milk anywhere in sight.

Her gesture had indicated that my father and I would sit on either side of the table and that she would sit at its head. As he sat down, my father looked slightly puzzled as if he did not understand the arrangement, but he quickly recovered and resumed conversation.

"How long has it been since I've seen you, Maggie?" he hollered. She returned to the dining room carrying a large tray. "Oh, I don't know," she answered. "It's been a long, long time, long enough for this to be the first time I've met either one of your children. So how long do you think that would be?"

"Ten years plus, I'd say." He craned his neck to get a better look at the tray she was carrying. As she placed it on the table, I could see a large bird whose feet were covered with white paper socks. The bird was surrounded by carrots, potatoes, broccoli, and a few other things I couldn't identify. All around the edges were sprigs of parsley, something I'd only seen once, at Thanksgiving.

"This looks like quite a feed," my father exclaimed, barely able to mask his increasing interest. He looked across the table at me for confirmation.

"It looks very interesting," I replied.

Maggie went back to the kitchen, but she returned quickly, carrying baskets of hot rolls and a water pitcher.

"Well, Maggie," my father said. "You certainly seemed to have changed since I last saw you. Grandmother told me you'd traveled before you took the teaching job here, but you're not the shy and retiring girl I remember. It's wonderful to see you in this new life."

She set the rolls on the table and began pouring us each a glass of water. "It's good to see you too, Bob, in your new life, with your lovely daughter. All I can remember about our last meeting was that you were the last cousin caught stuffing potatoes into Oscar Shotlander's tailpipe."

Momentarily speechless, my father blushed, but quickly recovered. "Touché," he replied sheepishly. "Good to be together again." In that moment, I thought I detected a note of sincerity that didn't always go along with his quick smile.

"Oh it is," she said with emphasis, "but I've forgotten something important." She hurried back to the kitchen, returning quickly, with a large steaming bowl of something else.

When she put an oddly shaped bowl on the table, my father used his loud praying voice to exclaim, "Gravy." He went on. "Shiny gravy with giblet bits. I couldn't be more pleased." He was smiling again, but this time he meant it.

"I've never seen anything like this before," I added truthfully, because the bowl had a pourer on one end and a handle on the other. We used any old bowl and a ladle. Where was the guy in the tuxedo?

"I'm happy you're pleased," she replied. "But let's eat before it gets cold."

For the next few minutes my father and I experienced rare moments of silence, as we remembered to chew with our mouths closed. We ate quickly, as we always did, and with enough gusto that Maggie was obviously pleased.

"It's a long drive," she said. "You must have been starved."

"Oh no, Maggie," my father responded with reverence. "We were hungry but we're just stunned into silence by the deliciousness of this meal. Aren't we?" He glanced in my direction.

I nodded, but no one was really looking at me.

"Well, I'm glad you like the meal, and I like seeing what we've all become! Next time," she said to me, "you'll have to bring your mother and brother."

"We will," I said much too loudly. "They'll like you too!" I added in a more grown up tone, noting that both Maggie and my father were laughing at my sudden outburst.

"And they'll love this gravy," my father added. "Wherever did you learn to make gravy like this? Quality like this is hard to find and says something very special about the woman who makes it."

"Oh, I didn't actually make the gravy," she answered. "I did learn to roast the chicken and vegetables, but the gravy is the newest thing. I got this gravy at the A & P. It comes in a blue can that I'll show to you. It's called "home-style," and your wife will be able to get it at any of the larger food stores. Perhaps she knows about it already."

33

"That's interesting," I said. In an instant, I saw hope for my future.

We finished the chicken, vegetables, gravy, and dessert and then talked for another two hours. Maggie seemed to know more than any grown-up I'd met about being in the fifth grade, and she was interested in my pets too. My dad said less and less, but he wasn't mad. I think he liked Maggie, and when we left, he asked her to visit us and said he really meant it! She said she would, and she thanked him again for the candy.

We got in the car, my father changed the radio dial to music, and began to sing. Miraculously, the defroster even started to work. The ride home was shorter and, as they say, "the rest was gravy."

The Dining Room

The old Roadmaster.

Sam Rizzo liked to say the he'd never been to Texas, but that he'd learned to build a ranch house just the same. He built a whole "allotment" full of them in a little town in northern Ohio that was far enough from his home town of Toledo to keep his shady reputation at bay.

My father bought one of the first two houses that Sam built. He moved our family into it when he moved to Ohio to take a job as a vacuum cleaner salesman. Sam moved into the other house with his new wife, Phyllis. Sam told my father that he left the bricks and mortar construction of the houses up to the building contractor but watched over the process carefully to be sure the contractor retained every element of the design that he had intended for the homes.

"Ranch houses are like dog biscuits," he told my father. "They're big on both ends and long in the middle."

Our house accurately reflected that design. With the garage on one end, two bedrooms on the other, and a long living room, dining room, and kitchen in between, the house could have looked like a dog biscuit if Mr. Rizzo hadn't added shingles, gables, and shutters to its white and stone siding.

"Inside the house," Mr. Rizzo added, "the secret is to have separate rooms, a special room for everything.

For instance, take the dining room. Having a separate dining room makes people feel rich. There might not be servants, but you won't be looking at a sink or a couch while you eat. You'll pay attention to a meal in a dining room, just like rich people do. It's uptown to have a dining room, a place dedicated solely to food and conversation."

Having said that, I don't remember a time when the Rizzos used their dining room for either fine food or conversation. Their housekeeper, Rosie, never fed them dinner in the dining room. Instead, they always ate at the red, stainless steel kitchen set that remained next to the sink in their kitchen for thirty years. When Rosie left town, the Rizzos moved their dining experience to the living room, eating endless frozen dinners on TV trays in front of the television. The times I ate there, they never talked or discussed anything during the meal except the choice of the meal itself. "Do you want a Birdseye roast beef dinner, fried chicken, or a turkey pot pie?"

However, at our house, during the good and the lean years, my mother set the table in the dining room. My father sat at its head, she sat at the other end, and my brother and I juggled positions regularly to take the side seat that was farthest from the kitchen. Unless something extraordinary happened, whoever lost this battle got to run all the kitchen errands for the duration of the meal.

We sat, we prayed, we ate, we talked. We talked and talked and talked. Mother made sure there were no open bottles, cans, or packaged goods on the table. Every morsel of food had its own glass dish or container. The idea was to act like the rich people, rich in pride if not in dollars, to prepare the children at this table with habits, manners, and traditions to make them feel comfortable in the finest social situations.

No matter that our fine food often consisted of potato and egg casseroles, overcooked pork chops, or an assortment of gray vegetables. Our dining room made us rich in time spent together discussing our world in a dog bone-shaped ranch house in northern Ohio.

Were there bigger places and issues to consider? Probably, but nothing that was much more interesting to the children of the household.

When guests came for dinner, my brother and I each got a guest on our side of the table. I always got the man, and my brother got the woman. That's how we learned to seat guests according to sex. Properly seated, the arrangement went "boy," "girl," "boy," "girl" until the table was filled. If there was a large number of guests, there were more tables, with children usually in the kitchen, arranged in the same sexist manner.

While the adults always made smiling references to us, guest dinners were not the time for childish conversation. We waited to be asked for an opinion while my father and mother discussed more adult issues with their peers. The exceptions to this rule involved special guests, and there weren't many of them.

My father's salesman friend, Jack Phillips, was one exception. Jack came for dinner whenever his travels brought him within dining range of our house. He was fat and short. He could have been Humpty Dumpty's shorter brother. His small round head was stuck to his body on the shortest neck ever called a neck. His eyes, held in small sockets, darted from object to object as though they were searching for a larger space. His nose was short, wide, and flat, but his mouth was big and wide. He grinned to punctuate every sentence. His hair was parted in the center and cut in a short military style. His fingernails were neatly trimmed. He smelled of fancy soap, and sometimes there was a hint of talc that showed above his shirt collar.

He always wore a double-breasted brown suit, a starched white shirt, and a wide tie with some kind of big, colorful geometric pattern on it. He wore brown wing-tipped shoes and shiny brown socks that always showed a pale piece of hairless leg between themselves and the cuffs of his pants.

When he walked into the house, he waddled from side to side and carried with him a special air, the air of Dutch Masters' cigar smoke. The cloud of smoke and Jack's cigar accompanied him everywhere, but he put the cigar away during dinner in deference to my mother. Jack knew that dinner was a serious issue with mother. He also knew he'd get more than one full plate of roast beef and gravy if he acted as though he was giving her dinner its due.

These dinners were fine with my brother and me. Besides getting a special dinner involving roast beef, we enjoyed listening to Jack and my father swap salesman stories about "the road."

Jack and my father often explained the perils of traveling to mother and to both of us. "It's harder to be on the road these days, Bobby," Jack would start. "With these new turnpikes and tunnels everywhere, every single truck in America is on the same road we are every day, day after day." He lost his grin and shook his head to give his words their full importance.

"You couldn't be more right, Jack," my father jumped right in. "And when those truck drivers get into those big rigs and get into those tunnels, they ride your as . . . I mean your bumper for miles, revving their engines. They drive me nuts."

Jack shook his head in agreement as he started to slice a potato. "All the time now, every day, day after day . . ." Unaware that he'd already begun to repeat himself, he started speaking with his mouth full. To emphasize his final words, he spoke more loudly, spewing a piece of potato into the gravy bowl as he reached the end of his sentence. My brother and I pretended not to notice, while my mother left for the kitchen, saying, "I'll think I'll just open the kitchen window for a little air." She deftly swept the gravy bowl off of the table and took it with her as she went.

The two men didn't miss a beat. "I know, Jack. "It's been bothering me, but this week, I finally found the answer."

Jack stopped eating altogether, looked up from his plate, and looked directly at my father, giving his full attention. "Well, do tell," Jack said. Those bas***d . . . bad men have had me talking to myself more than once."

Dad continued. "Last month, I was in the hill country and saw a big sign for fireworks. It wasn't even the Fourth of July, but there was a note on the sign. It said "special shipment" and the words were underlined. All the cars ahead of me pulled off to the side of the road. I did too, expecting something special."

Dad looked from side to side and lowered his voice, just as if he were afraid that Alan Funt was capturing it all for our favorite TV show, *Candid Camera*.

"That's right," he kept on, using the low voice. "This guy has an old table, and it's filled up to here." Dad had to stand up to show us how high. He started to sit down to continue, but mother re-entered the room.

"Do you need something, honey?" she asked as she and the gravy bowl returned to the table. She knew my father never got up from the table unless there was an emergency need for reinforcements from the kitchen.

"No, no," he said. "Just showing Jack and the kids something. The stack was that high, and it was made up of boxes and boxes of Super Colossal Cherry Bomb Blasters. I've never seen them here, but each one was just about the size of a golf ball, and each one had its own candlewick on the top. They were going like hotcakes, and I took a box just because I'd never seen 'em before and because I could get 'em."

"When I got back to the car, I thought I'd just gotten caught up in the moment, in the swarms of people wanting Cherry Bombs, but then as I got to driving I got to thinking they might come in handy. I started laughing at myself, but I knew what was going to happen when I got back on the turnpike. And things happened just as I thought they would."

"I was over in the mining part of Pennsylvania, the place where there were all the curves, and then finally that last long tunnel. Traffic was backing up, and I had a big red truck backed up behind me, shifting gears, revving his engine. Once he even honked his horn even though he could see all the cars in front of me. Ordinarily, I'd have been talking to myself, but on that day I just smiled to myself, knowing my patience would pay off.

"We went that way for about ten miles. I was hearing the revving and the shifting, looking in the rear view mirror, seeing the truck come within inches of my bumper. I kept smiling, but I took one of the super colossals from the box on the seat next to me and held it in my right hand just for luck.

"When I saw the tunnel up ahead, I took the next step and punched in the cigarette lighter. As we entered the tunnel, I slowed a bit to coordinate my plan and just about when I was half way through, I could see the grill of the red truck riding my tail. He had started to honk as he saw the other cars pull ahead of us, but he didn't fluster me."

Jack's eyes were getting bigger. His knife and fork were suspended in mid air.

"I rolled down the window with my left hand, holding the steering wheel and super colossal in my right." My father gestured, mimicking his moves. "Then I took the wheel with my left hand and moved the super colossal to that side also. I grabbed the cigarette lighter and managed to light the wick, grabbed the steering wheel with my right hand and dropped the colossal out the open window. I accelerated and waited for the few seconds it took."

He opened his left hand, and looked back as he spoke. When he looked back at us, he had begun to laugh as he talked.

"In my rear-view mirror, I could see the red truck was revving, shifting. I could see the guy's red face. He was waving his fist!"

"But then," he said as he roared with laughter, "Kabooom! Kabooom!"

We were all laughing and Jack was shaking his knife and fork above his head.

"Yeeees," Jack squealed. His face was red, and there were tears running down his face.

My father was crying too. He spoke between breaths. "You bet." He gasped, "That bas***d . . . bad guy . . . thought he'd blown every tire on his rig." He took a breath before continuing. "He pulled over right there at the end of the tunnel. I could see him getting out and looking under the truck, but I picked up my speed and just kept going."

Jack was still wheezing, as he grabbed his glass to take a drink of water.

"Oh, Bob," my mother interrupted gales of laughter, but she was laughing too. "That's awful." She repeated herself. "That's just awful. You could have given that man a heart attack."

"Better him than me," Dad said, still laughing. As he returned to his meal, we were still laughing too.

"I'll tell you one thing, Jack. I'm never traveling without those super colossals again. I'm just going to feel better knowing I have them."

"Dad, can we blow one up too?" My brother broke the rule prohibiting childish intervention, but no one seemed to mind. "I mean a real super colossal. All the kids will want to see it."

In an instant, my father's smile was gone. He looked directly at my brother and said in his most serious voice.

"Of course not, son. Super colossals are reserved for adult use only. You probably shouldn't tell this story. I was just trying to entertain Jack and your mother."

My mother moaned and got up to go to the kitchen again.

"Kabooom," Jack said shaking his head as he began to reach for another piece of meat.

I coughed twice to let out the laughter I knew should not come out.

"Cover your mouth with your napkin," my father directed. I used the napkin to cover the smile that hid behind it.

"We're just telling stories," Jack said. "Salesmen always tell stories."

"That's good, Bob." Jack took a bite and started a new story. "Now, let me tell you the one about the night Dickie Putzer got us kicked out of the Old Town Hotel in Lincoln, Nebraska, the night of the Schmelling fight."

"You children are excused," my mother said. "It's time to do your homework. Remember your manners and say goodnight to Mr. Phillips."

My brother and I left the table, but we could hear my parents and Mr. Phillips still laughing. Under the cover of their laughter, we both went through the back door to the garage. There, protected from all the elements, my father's Buick Roadmaster rested from its many travels. We looked through the window. There on the front seat was what looked like a shoe box, with a special label on one side.

"What does it say?" my brother asked.

"Super Colossal Cherry Bomb Blasters," I replied.

We walked out onto the driveway, laughing as we went.

"Nice night," a voice came from across the street. Mr. Rizzo was sitting on his front porch smoking his cigar.

Through the kitchen window, we could still hear Jack and my parents telling stories.

"It sure is, Mr. Rizzo," my brother said. We walked across the street to see him. Mother encouraged us to speak to the neighbors. As we got closer, Mr. Rizzo gestured to us to join him on the porch

"I could hear you all talking," he said. "When your Dad gets that excited, I can always hear him."

"Oh, I'm sorry, Mr. Rizzo. I'll get Mother to close the window. We don't mean to bother you," I said.

"Oh no, Honey. Don't worry. It's no bother at all. It's great to hear you all enjoy yourselves. That's when I know building that dining room was a good thing. Having conversations, friends, being together, those are good things. I always get a good laugh when you guys start talking around the table. They make up for the times I have to talk to people about cracks in their tile." Mr Rizzo took a big puff from his cigar, raised his head, and blew the smoke into the night air.

My brother and I tried to look at Mr. Rizzo as though we understood.

"Besides," he said, "I was with your father when he bought the Super colossals. It all happened just about that way, but we really bought them over in Monroeville from a friend of mine. He's a guy who can get certain things, and when your father was talking about those truckers, we just got this idea. He never really did ever tell me how they worked out. But now I'm going to ask him if I can ride along next time he knows he's going to take the Pennsylvania Turnpike. I'd just like to see those colossals work in person."

My brother and I didn't know what to say, so we said what mother always said: "Well, I guess it's time to do homework." We got up, hugged Mr. Rizzo and started to walk back across the street.

"Well, don't say anything to your folks," he said. "You guys never bother me. I don't mean to eavesdrop, but sometimes it's just funny. Like tonight," he said. "You remind me that life is a blast. Kabooom!" He gestured with his cigar, twirling its red tip above his head. Then he began laughing, laughing as hard as Jack Phillips, as hard as Dad, as hard as the rest of us had laughed. With his free hand, he reached into his pants pocket and pulled out a handkerchief. He couldn't stop laughing, even as he dabbed both eyes with his initialed white cotton pocket square.

We laughed again too, and the next night, my brother made a suggestion.

"Why don't we ask the Rizzos to dinner?" he asked. "We could eat in the dining room."

The First Time I Saw Paris

The Eiffel Tower, Paris, France

I first saw Paris in the Rizzos' basement
where painted murals hid stucco walls
masking mildew and Midwest discontent
with cartoon street scenes and poodle dog calls

Where painted murals hid stucco walls
the Rizzo's clipped, clownish dogs dance
midst cartoon street scenes and sharp poodle calls
Ohio sights and sounds mock tourist days in France

The Rizzos' clipped, clownish dogs dance
near the Seine, before the Eiffel Tower
Ohio sounds and sights mock one day in France
my dreams conjure life, luster and power

Near the Seine, before the Eiffel Tower
scenes masking mildew and Midwest discontent
help me imagine life beyond my own
when I first see Paris in the Rizzos' basement

The Blue Hole

The Blue Hole of Castalia, Ohio

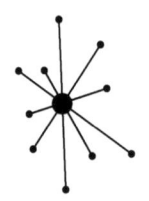

My parents took pictures of everything, and I have followed that model. The result is a basement filled with bins and boxes of photographs, some filled with organized albums, mostly random shots of feet, blurred animals, generations of children smiling through swaths of birthday-cake frosting. One old trunk holds all the old black-and-white photos, photos of people we don't know, photos of people our parents didn't know. To me these are the ones that hold the most interest because they leave everything to our imaginations.

I remember the Sunday afternoons my parents, my brother, and I spent going through these albums, stopping at pictures that were of interest, the few that were not a group of people standing in a row, sitting on the ground, or circled around a cake of some kind. These photos were fascinating. One featured an older male relative, who wore lederhosen and a felt feathered cap. He was holding what must have been a tasty treat over the head of a jumping deer. The photo featured the exact moment when the deer jumped, feet suspended in the air, as our relative directed a proud smile toward the camera.

"See, you had relatives that could make deer jump," my father noted. "That man had to be from your mother's side of the family. My side never had anyone that grand. Besides, we came from Canada, hardly a pair of lederhosen anywhere—even in Quebec—no lederhosen."

My mother rolled her eyes, going on to the next photo of a man laid out in a casket in front of a bay window. "Oh, I think that's Uncle Louie. He was a great uncle of your father's. We never knew him, but his name is written here." She pointed to the back of the photograph. "He was known for being a stiff long before his death, right, Bob?"

My mother and father were having a marvelous time. My brother and I were waiting for the time when the Sunday football game would be on TV.

My father shook his head. "What do you think these people were thinking when they took these pictures. Strange photos, I'd say."

"I don't think Uncle Louie was thinking about much," I laughed. Then my brother laughed. He laughed hard, always a good audience. My mother and father just smiled.

"Okay. You know what I mean. Someday, your children will be asking you about some of the pictures we took. They'll wonder about what we did. They'll think we were either stupid or boring too. I'm here to tell you, it will be up to you to make us appear interesting."

Years later, as I was looking through the picture boxes, his prophecy came true. As I began to sort the photos, my youngest grandson grabbed one photo and looked at it with great interest.

"Is this you, Nana? Boy you had lots of curly hair. What are you looking at? Are you looking into a lake?"

"That's the Blue Hole," I replied.

"What's the Blue Hole?" He looked puzzled.

"It's a big blue hole the size of a big pond. It's in Castalia,

Ohio, and it's supposedly the bluest, deepest pond in the country. No one has ever been able to tell how deep it is."

"Is the other side of the Blue Hole in China? What were you looking at? Are there fish in the Blue Hole? Crocodiles?" He laughed.

"No, nothing that exciting. I was looking for whatever it was that made my parents think we should visit the Blue Hole. I was looking for our reason to be there."

"Did you find it? The reason, I mean; what was it?"

I had found another photo of my friend Darla on the same visit to the Blue Hole, plumbing the depths, looking over a railing to get a better look. I handed the picture to Ryan.

"This is my friend Darla. She never let me forget that trip. Right here, she's asking me the same questions about the Blue Hole that you are. I told her to keep looking."

"Did anyone see what you were supposed to be looking for?" Ryan's eyes brightened.

"We both saw it, Ryan. We both saw the Blue Hole. The whole family had been in the car for an hour and a half to go see the Blue Hole. We spent an hour and a half going home too. We voted to say that when people asked us about the Blue Hole we would simply say, "I've never seen anything like it before."

That would be true. We had never gone that far to see so little, but we agreed not to tell.

"It's almost like the time Bapa and I took your mother and her friends to see a comet at 2:00 AM. People said seeing the comet was the chance of a lifetime, so we bought doughnuts, took our binoculars, and went out into the country for the two-hour time period they said it would appear. We looked and looked. But no comet appeared. Finally, we all took one more look at the sky, knowing that we had been shut out. However, having spent two hours looking, we were not about to be defeated. We ate our doughnuts, took a vote, and agreed to say 'we'd never seen anything like it before.'"

"Oh," Ryan said. "I get it. It's like the time we went down to the petting zoo where they only had one stinky goat."

"Exactly," I replied. "And you've never seen one like it since, right?"

"Right," he said. "I think I'll go and play with the dog."

I put the photos back in the boxes, thinking about how hard it is to throw any photo away. Even if a picture just has a foot on it, it's the foot of someone you know. Throwing it the trash feels almost be like performing an amputation. As a result, I think the photos in our basement will fill our daughter's basement one day. There will be no relief until the faded forms are filled exclusively with eyeballs and over-exposed ghosts. They'll remain mementos, providing some kind of emotional insulation, proving to future generations that they too had a legacy, no matter how odd, and that they too had this legacy to explain to their children.

"Twil ever be thus," 'tis said. 'Twil ever be thus until such time as there is a remedy for keeping what's past." (One time, I did hear a remedy for the inexplicable pictures. A speaker once said that when she found bad photos, blurs, or mixed parts, she'd simply enclose these shots with the billing statements she returned to utility companies. That way, she felt as though she had not betrayed anyone and that the people at the utility company would have a good day trying to explain this unexpected gift.)

Perhaps in the age of cell phones, it will be easier to delete bad photos, but it still will not be enough to explain the ordinary, silly pictures we take every day to suit ourselves.

It also won't be enough to explain the boxes of kid art, medals, trophies, and mementos that sit right next to the photographs or the tarnished silver wedding presents that stand next in line. Across the country, houses next to houses, the basements in all of them are filled with inexplicable treasures of former generations.

Will all of this come full circle in time? Probably not. Human beings are sentimental creatures. All of our stuff will probably just move on down the line. In the future, perhaps old video games and mutations of cell phones may replace the silver or photos. In any case, future generations also will fill their basements with things that have fallen out of favor. Our children will have their own explaining to do.

And the Blue Hole? It's still there, still blue, and still less than anyone imagined.

Rosie

Keeping an eye on things.

From the beginning, Sam Rizzo worried that his wife, Phyllis, would need both tending and watching. As a result, he gave Rosie Abruzzo to Phyllis as a wedding present. Rosie was designated as a homemaker/companion. Sam said that Rosie's role was to manage the household while keeping Phyllis on a straight and narrow path.

That's the explanation that Sam gave to my father when my dad asked him why the Rizzo's had Rosie and a regular cleaning lady. "Rosie manages the house," Mr. Rizzo said. "Rosie gives me confidence, let's me know what's going on. With Rosie there, I know someone's taking good care of Phyllis when I can't be there."

"Taking good care of Phyllis" was a big deal for Mr. Rizzo. When our family moved into our house on Central Boulevard, we walked across the street to introduce ourselves to the people across the street. The Rizzos were newly married, and Mr. Rizzo proudly showed us all the unique features that he'd built into his house just for Phyllis. "Phyllis is gorgeous," he said. "She's a girl that deserves special things."

He said those words as he took us downstairs into the basement of their house, showing us much more than the damp cinder-block walls that were in our basement. As we walked down the stairs, we saw scenes painted on the walls. Sam said the scenes were of Paris, a city that Phyllis had always wanted to visit. "I asked Phyllis, 'Why go there just once? I'll fix you something where you can be in Paris every day.'"

As we walked on into the basement itself, the transformation was a real eye-popper. There on the longest wall was a street scene of Paris, complete with couples walking poodles and the Eiffel Tower. On the wall directly adjacent to it was a little café scene complete with a soda fountain, café tables, and chairs. And at one of the nearby actual café tables, Phyllis and Rosie were seated, enjoying cokes and doing their nails.

"These are our new neighbors," Mr. Rizzo said as he introduced us to both women. Mrs. Rizzo looked like a movie star. She had what soap commercials touted as a creamy complexion, but she also had a beautiful blond hair and flaming red lips. Her eyelashes were long and dark, and her eyelids were smudged with purple, but when she smiled, all that showed were two bright eyes that were the color of robins' eggs. She was dressed all in pink, a fuzzy sweater, capri pants, and sandals to match. She was a real beauty all right, but she also turned out to be much more.

"Oh great," Mrs. Rizzo said. "You've got kids! They'll have to come over all the time and have sundaes." She looked directly at my brother and me. "You don't even have to bring your parents with you, just come on over. We have five different flavors of ice cream and four kinds of syrup. You can choose. Do you want a sundae now?" She turned and looked at Rosie.

"Rosie, dear, sundaes for everyone please. You all come over here and place your order."

As we moved toward the soda fountain, the older woman put down her nail file, stood up, and walked behind the counter. She was a small woman, who wore a white man's shirt untucked over tight black stretch pants. She was shorter than the 5' 2" that Mrs. Rizzo claimed to be. Her face was wrinkly, almost like a mummy's, but she'd used rouge and powder to try and hide the cracks in her face. She wore the same color of flaming red lipstick that Mrs. Rizzo wore, but the effect was far different. Her red lipstick smeared into the lines of her upper lip. Her eyelids were puffy. Her eyes were small, dark, intense, and almost hidden behind her wire-rimmed glasses. However, in contrast to her more than middle-aged appearance, Rosie moved quickly, energetically, and with purpose as she began preparing our sundaes.

"Vanilla, chocolate, strawberry, rocky road, or butter pecan?" she asked in a deep gravelly smoker's voice. She held an ice cream scoop in one hand and a sundae dish in the other and looked directly at my little brother.

"Chocolate with chocolate syrup please," he answered. "With a cherry if you've got some," he added.

As I gave my order, I noticed that Mrs. Rizzo had walked over to Mr. Rizzo and grabbed his hand.

"Oh, Sam, thank you for bringing me neighbors. Let's show them the rest of the house. The kids will love the living room. Rosie will take care of everything here, won't you, Rosie?"

"Sure, honey," Rosie responded, "but don't touch much with those nails. They're not dry yet."

It was then that I noticed Mrs. Rizzo's nails, nails to match her lips, nails that my mother later told me would not appear on the hands of any respectable woman. Rosie laughed as Mrs. Rizzo replied, "It's all right Rosie. If I nick one, we'll do them all again tomorrow."

With that comment, she raised her hand and used one red-pointed finger to show us the way upstairs.

As we went up the stairs and walked through the kitchen, I noticed there were red appliances to match Mrs. Rizzo's nails. As we went into the living room, I realized that we'd seen almost the only color we were going to see in the house. Everything in the living room was white—the rugs, the couches, the chairs, the TV console, and even white frames for the mirrors that hung on the walls. The dining room was the same, a white table, white chairs, and even a white chandelier. The only picture in the place was an oil painting of Mrs. Rizzo in a white dress. It was framed in white and hung above the white hutch, where white porcelain figures of horses and unicorns were scattered across the surface.

Lining the walls of both rooms were stuffed animals of all kinds. There had to be over one hundred of them, and they provided the limited amount of color that could be found on the upstairs floor of the house. Arranged in clumps of similar pastel colors, there were dogs, kittens, bears, and more stuffed versions of horses and unicorns. The whole place looked like a child's heavenly dream. For a minute, I felt like I was viewing heaven, on a tour of clouds. I never would have imagined the inside of the Rizzo's house from looking at its standard red brick ranch exterior.

As our whole family stood, stunned into silence by all the whiteness, a gravelly voice came from downstairs to interrupt our musings.

"Come and get 'em. Your treats are ready. Better get 'em before they melt and the cherries fall off." Rosie laughed as though she'd said something funny.

We returned to the basement, where my parents and Mr. and Mrs. Rizzo took their sundaes to one of the café tables and my brother, Rosie, and I took ours to the other. As my parents visited with the Rizzos, Rosie introduced herself to us in her own way. She produced a deck of cards and a pack of cigarettes. After lighting a cigarette, she placed it in her mouth where it dangled precariously as she talked. She never missed a beat and never lost any of the ash from its end.

"Here, pick a card," she said, as she fanned the deck and held the cards in front of us. As each of us made our choice, we began a long and wonderful relationship with the mysterious additional person who lived across the street. It didn't take long for her to be an attraction as big as the sundaes. She taught us card tricks, made cards disappear, acted like she found coins behind our ears, and always had time to listen to us. Most times, Mrs. Rizzo joined us and laughed as hard at the tricks and our reactions as Rosie did.

On our visits, my brother and I learned that Rosie did a limited amount of cooking, went everywhere Mrs. Rizzo went in the car, and always answered the door. Other than that, there didn't seem to be any chores for either of them. They ordered dinner from the Italian restaurant downtown, and the cleaning lady did the other chores on a regular basis. Mrs. Rizzo and Rosie did their nails, smoked cigarettes, and read movie magazines.

Rosie continued to teach us new games and tricks, and she gave us some advice about gambling. "Never bet more than you can afford to win. If you win too much, it will give you the itch for life—so be careful. Winning too much is the first step to losing big. That's something I wish someone had told me." Neither my brother nor I had a clue about the gambling part of her conversation. We just wanted to know how she always knew where all the cards were.

When I got to be the age where I learned that the purse I was carrying should match my belt and shoes, Rosie told me other things. She said a girl's lipstick and nail polish should match, noting that only women who had no aspirations neglected their nails. She also said it was often smart for a woman to act dumb. She added that the dumbest thing of all was to ask a question you didn't want to know the answer to. Finally, she told us that a good sense of humor was God's gift to us for dealing with the world. And she added, "That's why everything gets to be funny in the end."

Rosie's stay with the Rizzos ended when Mr. and Mrs. Rizzo brought their baby, Gary, home. "This baby is something I want to do for myself," Phyllis told mother. "I won't need watching with a baby at home, and I don't want to share him."

It didn't take long. No one knew if Rosie objected or even if she had anything to say about it. Nobody really had a chance to talk to her. Within days, a big black Cadillac parked across the street, and Rosie came out of the house carrying one large suitcase and one small one. She looked like a little old lady as she left, walking to the car wearing a black hat, suit and white gloves. She never looked back or waved at Phyllis, who waved good-bye to her from the doorway.

Rosie was gone. Neighborhood rumor had it that Sam had met Rosie when she was a madam for a house of prostitution in Toledo. She supposedly had gotten him out of some jams with his lowlife friends, and he'd repaid her with a job when she'd lost her business in a high-stakes card game. One of the neighbors said his arrangement with Rosie had been good for everybody. "She stayed away from the tables and Phyllis stayed close to home!"

We later heard that the small suitcase Rosie carried to the Cadillac upon her departure was filled with cash. Sam said the money was for all the good times and the bad ones too. He said he worried about Rosie losing it all. "Phyllis has the baby to keep her home," he'd said. "But Rosie's got way too much room. I'm sorry there's no way to help that anymore."

Years later, Gary, the Rizzo's son told me that Rosie had gone to Reno where she parlayed her money into a low-rent stable of prostitutes. "Laughin' Rosie's" was what the place was called, he said. I could hear Rosie's laugh as I remembered what she'd said: "After all, everything is funny in the end."

When Sam Rizzo died, the local priests refused to say mass for him or bury him locally. However, his nephew said that someone pulled some strings to get a priest in Toledo to conduct the funeral service and to bury him there, in consecrated ground. All reports were that the funeral turned out to be extremely small—Phyllis, Gary, Sam's brother, Leo, and a little old lady in a black suit, a little old lady who brought a bouquet of roses and laughed out loud when the priest said the part about "dust to dust."

The Last House in the Neighborhood

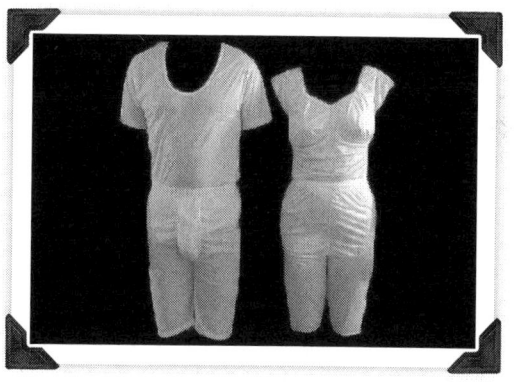

Morman garments.

* * *

The Fosters got the last house in the neighborhood, one of only six two-stories, with more bedrooms, gables, Georgian trim, and an all-brick exterior. It stood as a solid beacon of mid-American excess in the 1950's, but the house fit the Fosters perfectly.

All five of them, Paul and Marge, and their children, Jake, Martha, and Hope, were tall, square, rugged, blond, and blue-eyed, with all the right haircuts, clothes, and pets—two black Labradors named Mike and Millie and a cat named Priscilla.

Mr. Foster was an accountant. He wore a different colored tweed suit every day, as he drove his big Buick Roadmaster downtown to his new office, where a big sign hung over the door that listed his name and the accounting business. Mrs. Foster stayed home, of course, tending to Mr. Foster and the children. She attended all the PTA meetings to represent her shiny children and volunteered for leadership positions at the school in subsequent years. All the Foster children were good, but not great, students; however, they excelled in every sport that involved knocking down, running around, pitching harder, or throwing farther than any of their opponents. Not surprisingly, the beautiful family was welcomed

and instantly admired by their neighbors. They fit the bill in every way, down to their much coveted membership in the Elks Country Club. Except for the fact that no one knew which church they attended, the neighbors had all the essential information they needed to accept the family. However, when neighbors compared notes over drinks or coffee, they realized that no one had seen any of the Fosters at their church, even though everyone had seen them driving out of the neighborhood on Sunday morning in church clothes. Initially, this did not draw much attention, but around the holidays the neighbors seemed more curious,
and appeared relieved when the Fosters came home one day with Christmas decorations to put up in their yard. Still, no Catholics, no Methodists, no Lutherans, no Presbyterians, or members of the more contemporary churches had seen an Foster anywhere near their church.

I caught Bill Roley questioning the Foster's status one day when he and my dad were having a drink on the front porch. Bill asked Dad, "Don't you think it's strange that they never mention church?" "I guess it is, Bill. But how big a deal can it be? The Fosters are great—friendly, helpful—they keep their house up and they have Christmas decorations. To my mind, if a guy puts Santa on his front lawn, that's as good as saying that he believes in Jesus."

I moved along. The conversation was too weird even for me, but I did know one thing. The Fosters had a secret, and it was driving the neighborhood nuts. I don't think there was much more mention of the Fosters' church as they got more involved with the Elks Club, Girl Scouts, Boy Scouts, and other cherished local institutions. Everyone went on in an admiring fashion until one day my grandmother received afternoon visitors. Nana had been at home alone sitting on the front porch reading the paper when two young men wearing white shirts and ties came up the driveway. "Yes, lovely young men," she told us at dinner. "They wanted to introduce themselves, said they were guests of the Fosters and were on a mission to tell the story of their church. When I told them that your grandfather and I had been missionaries to the Indians in Traverse City, they were very excited. I told them I thought everyone should have a mission too." She scrutinized the likely heathens around the table and continued. "Lovely young men. Generous too. They gave me a book." She got up from the table, without being excused, and returned with a small bound book. "Here. It's a nice little book. A story about a journey. I think it's a book about the old West. You should read it." She kept nodding her head.

"Nice young men. I told you, guests of the Fosters." My dad looked at the book, smiled, and handed it to my mother. "The Book of Mormon?" Mom asked quizzically. "Yup," my dad said. "That's it. The boys go on a mission, and occasionally they stay with local families as they make their rounds. That's it. The Fosters are Mormons. I learned about them when I was selling car polish in Utah." "What are Mormons?" I asked. "Do they have a church?" In our town, Catholics were viewed as exotic by Methodists like us, and Jews were so rare that mostly we knew that they had no Christmas and the men wore those little beanies on their heads. The Fosters looked just like everyone wanted to look, and they were members of the Elks Club. If they had a church, it was probably cooler than ours. "Yes," my dad said. "They have their own church. Some people think the Mormons are a cult. They worship Jesus but think someone else is involved too. God talking to a prophet after Jesus. Stuff like that. Lots of them stick pretty much to themselves and they have lots of rules and don't eat or drink lots of things.

I heard some people say they wear funny underwear."
"Bob," my mother admonished over her glasses. "That's enough." "Do they have fun?" My little brother had stopped eating to ask his favorite question. "Sure," my mother said. "The Fosters have fun, don't they? They have a volleyball net. They play all the time." My brother smiled and nodded. Dad nodded, I nodded, my grandmother was still nodding. That was that. The Fosters were different, with different rules, but they still could have fun. Our family liked them, funny underwear or not. We had no more questions.

After the missionaries had visited, no one talked any more about the Fosters' church; however, the neighbors looked at them a bit more closely just to see. Mrs. Cornell said she'd seen some odd underwear on their clothesline, but I thought it look just like my grandmother's "garment." That's what she called her underwear; that's what they called their underwear too. Nothing new except for the age difference. However, the underwear question helped to set the tone for the neighborhood. Whenever the Fosters did something a neighbor didn't like, the neighbor would refer to it as "a Mormon thing" and move on. For the most part, that covered things sufficiently.

To this day, I don't know if any neighbors learned or knew much about Mormonism, but in our neighborhood people got along fine. The funny underwear remained the most fascinating difference between us. The Fosters' secret was underwhelming. As for the Fosters, they never said anything about Mormonism other than that their church was in Sandusky and that its real name was the Church of Jesus Christ of Latter-day Saints. Even this information was confusing. I heard my brother telling his friend that the name of their church was different "something about saints on ladders." The years have rolled along. Today, Marge Foster is one of the only original neighbors left alive, perhaps as a tribute to a healthy habit or two. However, the only thing I'd still love to know is what the Fosters thought about their neighbors. Did they feel we were different too?

The Little Black Bag

The story lies within.

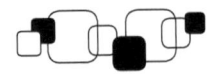

More than leaves fell around our house in the fall of 1953. My father fell off the ladder that he had used to climb up into the storage loft in our garage. Having retrieved two boxes of Lionel trains, he had taken two steps down from the loft, when the ladder legs slipped on an oil spot on the garage floor. In an instant, there was the sound of a quick slide, a loud yell, and a frightening thump as the ladder fell, and my father fell on top of it.

We all rushed to the door into the garage to see what had happened, knowing those noises were not good ones. When we opened the door, my father lay still, bleeding, with the box of trains still held tightly, safely in his hands. The trains were all right, but my father was not.

Mother shooed us back into the house and called the ambulance. I don't remember much more. It was a foggy time, with tears, sirens, and too much time to think. My brother and I wound up in the living room, on the piano bench that had held each of us up for more than a few lessons. During this crisis, we sat on the small bench, huddled together, hugging each other, brushing away tears, saying childish prayers, hoping someone was listening.

Our mother came into the room. We could see men in blue uniforms lifting my father into the ambulance. Mother was in a hurry. "You'll stay here with your grandmother," Mother said, as Nana entered the room, brushing her eyes with her handkerchief. "It will be all right," she said. "Daddy's strong, and he's awake now. He doesn't want you to worry."

Much later when she came home, she told us again that everything would be all right. My father had crushed the bones in his back, he'd have to stay at the hospital, he'd be in a cast, then he'd be fine. We were relieved. This time we cried happy tears, but as the saying goes, "It wasn't that easy."

While my father's recovery proceeded at the predicted slow pace, the needs of our household did not. Bills came, then more came, then, right on their heels, came second notices marked with red stamps.

My father had his own business as a salesman representing several different lines of automotive products. He worked "on commission," and when his accident put him "out of commission," things looked bleak. My brother and I sensed a new emotion in our parents. We felt their fear.

No matter that there was a parade of neighbors that came to our door, friends who brought casseroles, callers who offered to do errands and give rides. Even though my father's companies promised to stand by him, promised to send all the commissions that were generated by the territory to him, my parents smiled little and talked in the whispers that meant they had secrets that weren't meant to be shared.

I tried to be quiet, stayed out of the way, kept the volume down on our new TV, and went to school like nothing was happening. However, other people were too nice to us. Connie Shadley told me she was sorry we were having hard times when she brought her second tuna casserole to the kitchen door. When I returned her CorningWare® dish, she asked me, "What's your mother going to do?" I didn't know. I only knew I felt uncomfortable all the time.

When I asked my mother, "What are we going to do?" she said, in her most determined voice, "Your father will be fine. We'll all be fine. We just need a little time for healing. Then things will be just like they were before. Be patient and don't be afraid." I tried to believe her, but remember thinking that she was saying these things for herself too.

I determined that as the oldest child, I would say only kind things for the foreseeable future and work to be helpful. Cheery and helpful. It was the least I could do.

To that end, each night after dinner, I helped by doing the dishes. My grandmother took my brother for his bath, while my mother took dessert to my father as he lay in a hospital bed in the living room. We developed a routine, and began to act like things were normal even though there were still whispered conversations and stacks of mail at my father's bedside.

One Tuesday evening, things changed. The doorbell rang as I was drying the dishes. The door swung open with a loud "Hullo, anybody home?" even before I could make a move toward the door. The voice was that of Sam Rizzo, our neighbor from across the street.

Mr. Rizzo's black fedora hat led the rest of him into the back hall. He was wearing a dark blue double-breasted suit, a crisp white shirt, and a bright red and gold horizontally striped tie. His tie was held in place by a diamond-encrusted tie clip, and his diamond pinky ring flashed in the light, bringing attention to the fat cigar that he was holding. As he smiled and waved his cigar at me, I realized he also was carrying a small black bag.

"Hi ya, honey," he said. "I just thought I'd come over to give your daddy a little company. I heard a couple of jokes I thought he'd like. Do you think it would be all right if I just came on in?"

Mr. Rizzo was always a breath of fresh air. He had an aura of mystery about him. People said he'd been a gambler and pimp before he decided to "go straight" and build all the houses in our neighborhood. My father was one of the few people who liked Mr. Rizzo. Dad told people Sam was his friend, even when other neighbors gossiped about a shady past. In contrast, my mother wasn't so sure. She liked Sam's wife, Phyllis, but she still referred to the Rizzos simply as "neighbors."

In any case, I knew he'd cheer my father up. "Oh, go right in, Mr. Rizzo. Dad needs some new jokes."

"That's great, sweetie pie. I'll just go right on in." He patted me on the head as he passed. As he walked through the kitchen door, he turned his head around, smiled, and winked at me.

"Well, hello there, Bobby," his voice boomed as he moved into the living room.

I heard my mother say, "Sam, how nice of you to visit like this. Bob needs a little male company. I'll just go in and help Nana give Timmy his bath."

I heard her voice fade into the distance as she moved toward the other end of the house.

I put up the last dish, and moved to the kitchen table with the hope that I'd be able to hear everything. Mr. Rizzo was funny, but I'd have to eavesdrop to ever have a chance of hearing most of his jokes.

"Thanks for coming, pardner," my dad responded to Mr. Rizzo. He sounded happier than when he'd been talking with my mother.

Mr. Rizzo started right in. "Now, Bobby, I've got a couple of good jokes, but you're going to have to wait to hear them because I've been thinking about other things I want to discuss." I tilted my head to hear better.

"I just want you to know that you've always been a good friend." My father started to say "Sam," but Mr. Rizzo wouldn't let him speak.

"No, you listen to me," he continued. "You're the only regular friend I got, and I want you around feeling better. Now, I also know that doctors can only do so much when it comes to making you better. They can't hurry things up sometimes, and I know that for a business man like you that can create certain problems, if you know what I mean. I mean sometimes your financials can go all to hell and that can make you worry. It can get in the way of recovery. So I'm here, thinking perhaps I can be a friend to you. No strings, no interest, no nothing. I just want you to look in this bag and know that what's in it is yours."

I heard a small click as Mr. Rizzo opened his bag, and then I heard only silence. The silence was so silent that I almost went into the other room to see if anyone had died, but then there was a noise. It sounded like a gasp, then throat clearing. One, two, three times.

"Ahem, hmm." It was my father's voice. "Sam, that's just amazing." My father's voice was shaking. I thought he was about to cry.

"Ahem, hmm," he spoke again. "I want you to know that no one's ever done anything like this for me ever. "Ahem, hmm." He was at it again.

"I just can't, Sam. It's too much. It will be all right. I appreciate this but . . ."

"But what?" Sam said, confused. "There are no strings, Bobby. I can get more of this. If you need it, take it. Things happen. Friends help each other in the ways they can. This is my way."

There was another long pause. Then my father spoke again. "Thanks, Sam," he said. "I really mean it. It just happens,

I got good news today. The company is forwarding me all my commissions. The check will be a big one, big enough to take the worry away. You take the bag back across the street, and I promise I'll let you know if I ever need it. Now, tell me your jokes."

I had to see. I edged toward the living room as Mr. Rizzo started talking.

"It'll always be there for you, Bobby," he said. "And I'm leaving this blank check just in case. It's good for whatever you need. Use it if I'm not around to give you the bag. Now, did you hear the one about the traveling salesman who was working way out in Nebraska . . . "

I peeked into the living room. Neither man noticed, but I saw what I came to see. There on the table next to my father's bed, the black bag lay open. I could see money, stacks of bills wrapped in rubber bands. There were enough stacks to fill the bag. It was a modern day treasure box laid wide open in our living room.

I put my hands over my mouth to keep from making the noise that was caught in my throat. I went back to the kitchen, got my homework from the counter and sat down to act like I was doing something.

Mr. Rizzo and my father talked on for another hour, laughing loudly. When Mr. Rizzo left, he came through the kitchen. He already had his hat and coat on and was still carrying what was left of his burnt-out cigar in his hand with the pinky ring. He patted my head again as he went by, and I could see that he was carrying the black bag in his other hand.

"Night, honey," he said. "Take good care of your daddy, and tell your momma 'bye' for me. I can't tell you the jokes I told your daddy, but I'm going home to find a good one for you right now." He waved and winked again as he left.

I sat there, stunned, still doing nothing as I heard my mother talking to my father. "My God," I heard her say. It was the first and only time I heard that exclamation.

When I went through the living room to go to bed, I visited with my father and mother. Dad simply said, "Sam Rizzo is a good friend." My mother shook her head. She looked stunned, said she was thinking, said she didn't really know what to think. What happened that night in our living room was never mentioned again.

In the weeks that followed, my father's commission checks did come. The people in his territory had called in orders to help him. He came out of his dark days and got back to normal just as the doctors had predicted. Throughout his ordeal, Sam Rizzo came to visit every Tuesday and often on other days as well.

My mother spoke more to Mr. Rizzo. When my father felt better, she even called Phyllis up. I heard her say, "Bob's feeling a little better now, Phyllis, and I can't think of anything that would cheer him up more than having some of our good friends over for dinner. Do you and Sam have any plans for Saturday night?"

Spring

Baby gets a new ride.

It was June, the ripest month of spring, and everything was blooming. Hard-to-grow azaleas appeared in our front yard in their showiest shades of red. A cardinal's nest appeared between the yellow stalks of the forsythia bush that framed my bedroom window. Next door, the Fullers' cat, Tootsie, had kittens; across the backyard alley, the Doublos' Dalmatian had four randomly spotted puppies; and across the street, the Rizzos packed up their salmon-and-white convertible and went to Florida to buy a baby.

I was twelve, and generally uninterested in either the rites of spring or neighborhood events. But on the day the Rizzos left town, I was perched on the wall in front of our house, drying my hair in the sun, and reading *Teen* magazine. I sat in the direct line of sight for events that were transpiring across the street, and I couldn't help but notice.

Initially, there was lots of scurrying. First, Mr. Rizzo came out of the house with one of Mrs. Rizzo's big white suitcases. Then, even before he could reach the trunk of the Oldsmobile convertible that sat on the driveway, I heard her calling after him.

"Sam, honey, let me put just a couple of things in there." She came through the back door in a hurry, dressed in her full summer whites. From bottom to top everything was white—platform shoes with lots of straps and open toes, tapered toreador pants cinched with a thick belt, a shiny blouse with a scooped collar and puffy sleeves. She topped everything off with a white scarf tied around her neck. In her right hand, she carried a pair of big white-rimmed sunglasses and in her left hand, an extra pair of white shoes and a lacy white something else.

She talked so loudly that I looked right over the top of a *Teen* picture of Frankie Avalon to see her pop open the suitcase in the middle of the driveway. As she jammed all the clothes that spilled onto the sidewalk as well as the extra shoes and the white thing back into the suitcase, she kept talking.

"We'll need at least one diaper to get started," she said. "I'll need more comfortable shoes too. I think babies take a lot of walking."

Suddenly, she stood up straight, put one hand on her hip and waved at me with the other.

"We're going to Florida, honey! We're going to get a little baby boy, and bring him right back here, right back here where you can see him, touch him, and even babysit if you want to. He'll be just like another little brother to you. What do you think?"

I dropped my magazine, and started fiddling with my hair. I was stunned. No one had told me that spring was going to bring any more than a few new birds, kittens, and puppies to the neighborhood. Mrs. Rizzo's twist of a new baby was a whole new shocking development. The Rizzos had been married all the seven years we'd lived in our house, and there had never been any talk of a baby. Since she always referred to my brother and me as her "adopted" children, I thought that was it. We were her baby substitutes. I'd never considered anything else.

"Wow," I hollered, loudly enough to shock myself. I stumbled for words and stammered until I found the phrase that I still use when I'm dumbfounded enough not to risk an opinion. "That's really something." I jumped off the wall, ran across the street, and opened my arms to hug her.

"Well, we just got the call. It can't have been more than a half an hour ago, so Mr. Rizzo and I are in a dither, but we're going to get right in the car and go. We've been waiting for this call all of our lives."

Mr. Rizzo nodded in agreement. He'd been standing there all the time she'd been talking, puffing on his cigar and twisting the ring on his little finger.

"Yes," he said. "This is the call we've been waiting for. It's been so long, we thought it might never come."

Mrs. Rizzo was still hugging me. When I looked up, I could see streaks of tears on her face even as I felt a big wet drop right on my forehead. Mr. Rizzo bent down, picked up the suitcase, and moved to the back of the car.

He looked good too as he stood in the driveway wearing his spectator wingtips, black and white, along with shiny gray slacks. He wore a silky gray shirt and a broad black-and-white checked tie, held close to his chest by a diamond-studded tie clip. Both of the Rizzos had dressed up to go and get their new baby.

While Mrs. Rizzo and I stood there, he walked back to us, reached into his pocket and handed her his handkerchief. Then he looked at me again.

"It's a big day," he said. "But we're just going down and coming right back. It shouldn't take more than a few days. We don't want to hang around Florida when we can get that little guy back here to his new home."

"If you'll just ask your mom and dad to keep an eye on the house, we'll appreciate it. This has all happened in such a hurry. Your mom will really be surprised when she gets home from the hair shop and find us gone. I know she's got a key . . . "

"Oh, don't worry, Mr. Rizzo," I interrupted him. "We'll take care of everything. I mean, a new baby. I just didn't know, and this is such a surprise and so exciting."

It was his turn to interrupt. "Well, Phyllis, we've got to get going. I'll get my bags, and you check to see if we've forgotten anything. Gotta make good time to Florida, you know." He rubbed the top of my head and walked back into the house.

Mrs. Rizzo hugged me tight once more and then let go of me. "We're starting all over again" she smiled. "We're starting all over again with a new baby." She blew me a kiss as she followed Mr. Rizzo back into the house.

I walked back across the street to my house and climbed back onto the wall. I picked my magazine up, pretending to read, but the things that were happening on my street were bigger than news flashes about Dion DiMucci's new girlfriend.

As the Rizzos came back out of the house, I noticed that Mrs. Rizzo had put on her dark glasses and some kind of fishnet headcover to keep her hair in place. Mr. Rizzo carried a large brown suitcase and a smaller black one that looked like a doctor's bag. It was the one he took when he made trips to the bank.

Mr. Rizzo put the bags in the trunk of the car while Mrs. Rizzo got settled in the front seat. Mr. Rizzo slid into the driver's seat, adjusted the rearview mirror and started the car. Mrs. Rizzo looked into the mirror on the visor and fixed her lipstick. They were ready to go.

When they backed out of the driveway, they looked my way one more time and waved. Mrs. Rizzo blew me another kiss. They were gone . . . on the way to Florida, on the way to starting a whole new life.

My mother got home about a half an hour later. I was still sitting on the wall, staring at the Rizzos' house. I'd given up pretending to read. I just kept thinking about the Rizzos and how quickly the world across the street had changed. My mother's return brought me back into the afternoon.

"Hi," Mom said, but she looked puzzled. "What are you doing out here, and what happened to your hair?"

I reached for my head, having forgotten the drying process. My hair was completely dry. I'd forgotten to run inside and put on the large hairy pink rollers that kept it straight. The effect of forgetting was obvious. My hair had sprung into a frazzled, fluffy hairy halo of curls.

"You've either decided to try out for the circus or you've seen a ghost," Mom joked as we went inside.

"You won't believe it," I said shaking my head. "The Rizzos have gone to Florida to get a baby."

"What?" my mother exclaimed. She almost ran into the kitchen door as she looked around at me, but this time she was the one who looked like she'd seen a ghost.

"No kidding," I said, as I tried to tamp down my hair with both hands. "I was waiting for my hair to dry, heard all the commotion . . ."

We both sat down at the kitchen table, where I filled her in on everything. Once I started to explain about the call and the half hour, Mom settled in and told me that the Rizzos had been trying to adopt a baby for quite some time. She said they'd been turned down several times, and Mrs. Rizzo had been heartbroken, maybe even depressed. Mom said Mrs. Rizzo had been working to accept the fact that they weren't going to get a baby, but she said that Mr. Rizzo had told Dad there might be one more option. She had no idea what that meant or how things had worked out, but she was glad the Rizzos were going to have the child they'd wanted. Mom added she'd keep an eye on the house and suggested that I should try to do something with my hair.

"Use the rollers right away this time," she laughed, as I walked toward the bathroom to take another shower. As I was in the process of trying to drown my hair, I thought of Mrs. Rizzo's words about starting over again, and I promised myself that if I ever had the chance to do things over again, I'd like to do those things with different hair.

After showering and getting the big pink rollers firmly into place, I went back into the kitchen to reward myself with a Coke®. My father had gotten home from work, and now he and my mother were at the kitchen table discussing the Rizzos.

"What's wrong with your hair?" my father asked, as I stuck my curler-coiffed head into the refrigerator to get my Coke®. I didn't answer. Instead, I sat down at the table to get back into the conversation.

"Dad, what do you think about the Rizzos? How do you think they got the baby in Florida? What do you know about the baby?" I tried to get all my questions in at once.

"I think the Rizzos really want a baby," my dad said. "They're our friends and I'm happy for them. They've had trouble getting a baby, and I think they'll appreciate having this chance. I hope they don't have any trouble."

"Why would they have trouble?" I asked.

"Oh, I don't know. I was just talking," my father said. "What do you think we'll be having for dinner?" Clearly, the subject was closed.

I rolled my eyes, knowing I'd been dismissed, gave it my best twelve-year-old sigh, and went back out the door to retrieve my magazine. When I approached the wall, I realized the kitchen window was open. I hung around, opened my magazine, and pretended to read an article about Annette Funicello, but I was listening for whispers from within. I wasn't disappointed.

"That's right," my dad said softly to my mother. "Phyllis was depressed about being dumped by the last adoption agency. She said that she needed a baby to feel like a woman. She said a baby was the only thing she really wanted in life, the only thing that would help her to get over not being able to have one herself. He said he knew it was his fault and that he'd get her a baby. No matter what, he'd get her one.

"Sam was beside himself when he told me, but he said he knew people in Florida, who had put him in touch with a doctor who could help. He said this doctor helped people like him, who'd been rejected by agencies. The doctor said that the Rizzos could get a good healthy baby if they could afford it. He needed to have cash on hand. He got the cash and stashed it in the freezer, while they waited for the call."

My mother didn't say much, just "Poor Phyllis," but my curlers and I were about to explode. Did this mean the Rizzos were buying a baby? This sounded like a weird deal to me, one that defied all the theories of reproduction and baby-making that I'd heard. After health class, we'd laughed at kids who thought that Angela Aleana had gone to the store to buy her baby when she got pregnant and had to leave school. Now, the Rizzos were buying a baby, and I wanted to understand.

My parents decided I didn't need to understand. We didn't talk about the Rizzos or the baby until the day their convertible drove into their driveway, slowly, and with the top up. We all ran out of the house and acted like it was the biggest holiday of the year! What's more amazing is that we all acted as if this were normal.

I had mulled over so many questions about the baby while the Rizzos were away. What might the baby cost? Was it a bargain baby? How did the baby's real mother feel? How could she take money for her baby? How was Mrs. Rizzo going to take care of the baby when she spent so much time at the beauty parlor? Could anyone of more than average intelligence see Mr. Rizzo as a Little League coach?

All these questions remained when the Rizzos drove into the driveway, but as we ran across the street to greet the Rizzos, my mother was crying, and suddenly I was too! In what seemed to be slow motion, Mr. Rizzo opened his car door and ran around the car to open Mrs. Rizzo's door. He bent over, reached in and lifted out a wiggly blue bundle. Mrs. Rizzo began to get out of the car, and as she did, Mr. Rizzo held the bundle high in the air, above his head, as if he were holding a trophy of some kind.

"Gary's home," he shouted. "Our baby boy is home. Come see our beautiful boy."

My questions were gone. Hardly anyone could say anything. We were all laughing and crying together, looking at the little dark-eyed, dark-haired baby that looked out at us from the depths of his blanket. I wondered what his questions would be. After all the adults got their chance, Mrs. Rizzo handed the baby to me. Everyone was still talking at once.

"Do you know you're home?" I asked in a whisper. "Do you know you're beginning an all-new life?" I hugged him close.

Later, I saw Mr. Rizzo unloading the car. There were just two suitcases. The little black valise was missing. Mr. Rizzo whistled, and his diamond pinky ring flashed the last reflected light of the setting sun. He picked up the suitcases, took a last look at the sunset and walked through the back door of a suddenly new home.

Coffee

Magical meetings.

Coffee was more than a drink in our neighborhood. It was a ritual. Each day, after the men went to work and the children left for school, neighborhood doors slammed up and down the street as selected women poured out of their homes to go to coffee.

While coffee was always served at these gatherings as the warm dark caffeinated morning liquid of choice in the 1950's, no one came to coffee because it was good to the very last drop. No, the carefully selected neighbors who came to coffee came to talk, to talk about their husbands, their children, and the other neighbors. Occasionally, the women shared a recipe or a household hint, but stories and secrets were what made coffee more powerful than caffeine. Coffee was the force that maintained the expectations and standards of the neighborhood.

I learned all of this when I came home sick one day when my mother was the hostess for "coffee."

As I walked in the back door, with a note in my hand from the school nurse, I was greeted by the five main players in the coffee klatch: Alma Fuller, Paula Rothy, Belle Hamlin, Ellen Chapman, and my mother. Phyllis Rizzo, from across the street, was notably absent, as was our next-door neighbor, Ray Anne Bosch.

"What's wrong?" Mother asked even before I could get through the door.

"Mrs. Lucal says I have a temperature. Miss Prunty sent me down to her office after she told the whole Spanish class that I was sneezing so much that I was disrupting the lesson." I offered my mother the whole story as I handed her the written note.

"I'm sorry," she said as she got up and put the palm of her hand across my forehead. "Yes, you are warm. You'd better change your clothes and get into bed. I'll pour everyone another cup of coffee, and then I'll be right in to check on you."

"Sorry you're sick, honey," Mrs. Rothy said. Mrs. Rothy always was nice, but the others chimed in too. They always said something nice when Mrs. Rothy did because they all wanted everyone to think they were as nice as Mrs. Rothy.

"Thanks," I said, as I moved out of the kitchen and into my bedroom. As I went into my room, I thought about closing the door, but I left it open, knowing that if I had to be in bed, their conversation would be my only form of entertainment.

When Mother came in to check on me, I already had gotten into bed. She brought me water and set it on my nightstand. "Try and sleep," she said. "It's the only way to nip a cold in the bud."

"I'll try," I said. But as she was closing the bedroom door, I said, "Mom, it gets so hot in here, just leave it open."

"We won't keep you awake?"

"Oh, no," I answered. I felt better already, knowing I'd miss all of geography and a math quiz in the afternoon. I'd passed the need for a nap.

"She'll be fine in the morning," I heard Mother say. "I'll keep giving her fluids and will make sure she rests."

"Lots of that going around," I heard Ellen Chapman's voice. "Now, where were we?"

Belle Hamlin answered, "We were talking about Marie Shadly. Bebe Gross told me that Marie is divorced. Eddie isn't really Harry's after all."

"That's a relief," Alma interrupted. I heard laughing.

"Of course, Bebe's divorced too. You never know," Belle added.

The conversation continued in this vein. I learned that everyone thought the Rizzos' new convertible was the wrong color. "Salmon's not the color of a car," Alma said. "It's the color of a fish."

"I don't like the color of the Abruzzo's house either." I couldn't tell who was talking. "That baby blue makes it look like something right out of the nursery."

"Well, they're Eye-talian, you know." It was Alma again. "And you know in Eye-talian everything's got to be too much. Have you ever been to an Eye-talian funeral? You'd think they were the only ones that ever had a death in the family. All that wailing. I went to one where the widow even jumped into the grave."

"NOOOO . . ." a chorus of voices responded.

"I swear to God," Alma replied.

"Next subject." I heard my mother's firm voice.

"How about the PTA?" I heard Belle ask. "Who should we nominate to be president?"

That's the last I remember. In fact, the PTA conversation did put me to sleep. The next thing I remember is my mother coming back into the room to check my temperature. As she put her hand on my forehead, I asked, "Mom, I heard Mrs. Chapman say 'swear to God.' What was that all about, and the thing about the Rizzos' car?"

"Oh, lots of things get said at coffee, honey. Sometimes people say more than they should or mean to, but they're all good friends and neighbors."

"Does everyone get invited to coffee, Mom? I mean is Mrs. Rizzo invited? How about Mrs. Bosch?"

"They've all been divorced, sweetie, and that makes lots of people uncomfortable. I see them at different times. Most times, they can't come to coffee. Besides Mrs. Rizzo usually comes over after lunch. I see her every day too."

"But are they invited to coffee or not?" I asked again.

Mother said, "Don't get excited. I'm going to make you some soup. Just rest now." She walked out of the room without answering me.

After lunch, the day dragged on. I fell asleep again listening to the sound of the vacuum cleaner, but I woke up quickly when the doorbell rang. Before it finished ringing, I heard a voice holler, "Yoohoo, DeeDee, it's me."

Mrs. Rizzo had arrived for afternoon coffee. She often was seated at the kitchen table when I got home from school. I wasn't surprised to hear her voice, but I was surprised to see her standing at my bedroom door.

"Can I come in, honey?" she asked as she tiptoed into the room. "I know you're resting, but Paula told me you came home from school, so I brought you something." She held up the *Photoplay* magazine she'd been hiding behind her back. "It's the latest edition. It's got all the stars in it and a new fold-out picture of Frankie Avalon. It's just the thing for a girl that's not feeling too great."

I sat straight up in bed. *Photoplay* was a magazine for teenagers and women. Right then and right there, Mrs. Rizzo and Frankie Avalon were advancing my metamorphosis into adulthood.

"Wow, Frankie Avalon!" I knew Mrs. Rizzo could tell that I was cheering up.

"Yes, I like him too! He's Italian, you know, like Mr. Rizzo. He may not be tall, but he is dark and handsome." She covered her face and giggled. For a moment, she reminded me of my friend Darla.

Mother came into the room. "Hi, Phyllis." When she saw the magazine she acted puzzled, but she managed to say, "How nice of you. Just the sort of thing to cheer a girl up." She looked my way and winked. "Let's go have some coffee."

"Sure, DeeDee. That'll be great. You get some rest, okay? Get some rest right after you read the story about Frankie Avalon." She walked into the kitchen with my mother. Thankfully, they left the bedroom door open.

"I've got something to tell you, DeeDee." Mrs. Rizzo had lowered her voice, but I could still hear.

"I'm sorry to say that Sam and I are having some troubles. Gary's gotten into some trouble in school. They say he's playing with the girls' toys. Apparently he doesn't get along with the boys. Sam's mad at me, says it's my fault, but Gary's just a sweet boy. I don't think there's any harm. Do you? Anyway, Sam's saying we need money so he's going to Reno. He's going back to the gambling, and I hate that. He's says he's going next week. He doesn't know when he'll be back, but wants this thing with Gary to be fixed by the time he gets home . . . I just don't know. The neighbors will all go nuts. They talk about us anyway, and maybe when they know Sam's left town, they won't even let their kids play with Gary. Pammy Bosch is the only one, the only one he ever wants to play with, the only one that can come over."

Then it was quiet. I heard small noises. I even thought I could hear Mrs. Rizzo crying.

I craned my neck toward the kitchen to see. Through the open door, I could see my mother hugging Mrs. Rizzo.

After that day, things changed for our neighborhood. The next day, Mr. Rizzo took the Salmon-colored convertible to the airport. He carried two big bags, but he didn't carry any little ones. He looked hunched over as he put the bags into the car, and when the car pulled out of the drive way, he didn't wave or even look across the street.

The next week, Gary Rizzo got sent home from school. I heard that the note the school sent home to Mrs. Rizzo said Gary needed counseling.

Mrs. Chapman called to ask if my mother could have coffee. She said she had news. My mother told her that she'd have to miss coffee. She said she was sorry but that coffee made her nervous. She told Mrs. Chapman to call her if there was any good news.

In the months that followed, Mother spent more time with Mrs. Rizzo. She said Phyllis needed some help. When I'd get home from school, there often was a note on the kitchen table. "Having coffee with Phyllis" was usually what it said.

One day there was a card in the mailbox from Mr. Rizzo. There was a picture of a building that was lit with lights. The sign on its front said "Harrah's."

Mr. Rizzo's wrote "Hope everything's good in my neighborhood. Take care. Hope to be home soon." On the back of the card, the script was shaky and hard to read.

Halloween, 1953

Polio.

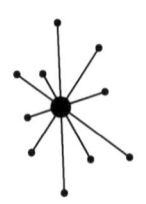

With all of its orangeness, hollow-eyed masks, rubber rats, and rag-swathed mummies, Halloween adds the final exclamation point to the month of October. However, the surprises that came to our house that year did not involve any feigned apparitions. They involved something more sinister, more inexplicable, a terrifying specter of disease. How did it come into our house? Under the door, from rainwater, from an unsuspecting friend? We did not know, but it came anyway.

Initially, it seemed ordinary, a stiff neck, a swollen gland, a cold coming on. But then it revealed itself when my brother's chin could no longer touch his chest, and a weakness in one leg created a limp when he went to his room after saying he was going to bed. It was only 6:30 p.m., it was 1953; it was five days before Halloween when it came to our house.

Dr. Lynn came right away. He walked in through the front door with his black bag, in one of his tweed suits, smelling of pipe smoke, bringing the aura of confidence he always shared with his patients.

"Well, let's see," he said, as he put down his bag and rubbed his hands together. He rubbed his hands together before he ever touched anyone, and he rubbed the top of my head, as he listened to my mother's description of my brother's movement, his glands, his tiredness. I really didn't listen; I just felt relieved. Dr. Lynn always knew how to make things better. He was handsome, spoke softly, and reminded me of the doctor in the picture that hung in his office. The photo was famous—a doctor sitting at the bedside of a child patient. It could have been any doctor, but I was sure it was Dr. Lynn.

"Okay," he said. "Let's go in to see Timmy. He might be more comfortable if he just stayed in his own bed."

They went into my brother's bedroom. I heard the doctor talking. "I'm going to feel your neck, Timmy," he said. "I hope my hands aren't too cold."

"They feel good," Timmy said. "I'm so hot, so hot." He started to cry.

I didn't want to hear anymore. I went into the dining room and sat at the table. I was alone. My grandmother, who lived with us, was sick too. She had a kidney infection and had to stay in bed. My dad had to sit in a special lounge chair in the living room because he was still in a cast from his fall from a ladder. He was very quiet, and really wasn't paying attention to me anyway. To say the least, October had been a bad month. Mom and I were the only ones left on our feet, but I tried not to worry.

"Timmy makes a big deal of everything," I kept repeating in my head, even as I heard the doctor and my mother going into the living room to talk with my father.

"Just a cold," I whispered to myself as I moved closer to the door to eavesdrop.

"This isn't good," the doctor said. "His fever is almost 103, he's not very stable on his feet, and his glands are greatly enlarged. There's obvious weakness in his neck. I will have to take some blood, but this is probably something involving his nervous system. It could be meningitis or it could be polio. Believe it or not, it would be better if it were polio."

There was no big response from my parents, but I did hear my mother say, "It will be all right, Bob, really. It has to be. It will be all right."

My father only said, "I know," but his voice was shaking.

I began circling the table, going round and round, faster each time, not believing, but scared, really scared, and no one even seemed to know where I was, if I'd heard. All I could think of was the word POLIO. It meant strange metal tubes filled with people, it meant kids in wheelchairs, it meant metal braces. It was the worst, the scariest thing I knew about. There was nothing you could imagine for Halloween or in real life that would be scarier.

Would Timmy be like that? Could he stay home? Did he have to leave? Then came the final question, "Am I going to get it? What's going to happen to me?" Again and again, I asked the scariest question as I buzzed around the dining room table.

"What's going to happen to me?"

I took a breath and almost bumped into Dr. Lynn and my mother.

"Am I going to get it?" I cried, and grabbed my mother around her waist.

I felt Dr. Lynn's hand on my head as he said, "You're a brave girl, and you're probably not going to get anything. I'll bring some medicine tomorrow to help you stay healthy. Don't you worry. Just help your mother and dad, and we'll take care of both Timmy and you."

My mother said, "I'm sorry, honey. We were talking too loud. I meant to tell you about this is a different way. We'll all be fine," she said. "We just need to take care of Timmy now. You can stay with Nana and Dad, and I know you'll be a big help to them."

She sounded sure as she sent me to bed. "It will be all right," I said to myself as I got into bed. "Mom, can I go and see Timmy for a minute?"

"No, honey," she said. "You can't be together for a while. He'll have to go to the hospital, but I'll be able to tell you more when you wake up tomorrow. You won't be going to school so sleep in. And I'll see you a little later." I couldn't believe it, but I was sleepy. I drifted off, thinking "it will be all right." Mother said so, I know so, and besides, Timmy's only four, it's too soon for him to die.

The next morning, when I woke up, my dad told me that mother and Charlie Moore had taken Tim to a hospital in Cleveland. Charlie was our neighbor who sold cars. He was tough, bragged a lot, and generally thought he was a big deal. Everybody said so, but he'd agreed to drive my brother and mother to Cleveland.

Dad said that Mom did not want Tim to go by ambulance, didn't want him to be too scared, so Charlie drove, even though he had three girls at home. He'd told my dad that he couldn't go yet, not in the body cast. Many years later, my mother told me that Charlie had said, "Robert, you're not going anywhere. We don't need two people in the neighborhood to worry about. I'll take DeeDee, and we'll try to get things settled before you arrive on the scene."

"Will Timmy have to be in one of those iron tubes?" I asked.

"I hope not," my father replied. Then Dr. Lynn was at the front door, and it was my turn to get a shot of gamma globulin, the only recommended treatment to prevent polio in the early Fifties.

The shot made me feel better. I felt protected. My mother came home and said that Timmy did not have to go into one of the tubes. When she said "he'll be fine" another time, I'd heard it often enough to begin to believe it.

She did tell me we were in quarantine, which meant we could not go anywhere or have anyone over except Dr. Lynn. When I asked about Charlie Moore, she said Charlie had been a big help, but he couldn't come over for a few days either. (Again, years later, she told me Charlie Moore had burned his clothes when he got home from taking Tim to the hospital and had his car fumigated the next day.)

My mother drove back and forth to the hospital, and sometimes my father went, but Halloween was coming and I was becoming concerned. What could I do? We couldn't give candy away—we'd have to tell people why—worst of all, I knew this meant me missing trick or treating altogether.

When my mother and dad got home one day and said Timmy was doing better, I posed these concerns to them. Halloween was becoming a serious question for me.

"It will be a different Halloween," my mother said. You won't be able to trick or treat, but I may have something that will work as a costume." She went into my father's closet and took one of the long paper wrappers that used to cover dry cleaning on the hanger and brought it to me.

"Here," she said. "Why don't you use your crayons and your imagination to create a costume? We can paste things on it if you like, and maybe Nana will help."

So for the two nights before trick or treat, my much-recovered grandmother and I colored and pasted things onto the paper bag. The final product sported dots, spots, and a pinned-on yellow collar of feathers taken from a ripped stuffed duck.

I hung the bag on a hanger until trick-or-treat night. I donned my costume and rubbed lipstick on my nose and lips to heighten the clown effect of my self-made wonder.

When it began to get dark, we turned the light on as usual, and the trick-or-treaters came to our front steps. My father stood behind me, ready to coach me if I got the script wrong, but I got it right.

I opened the door in full costume and said, "I'm sorry we can't give you anything tonight, but we are under quarantine. We have POLIO here."

With that, all the children, no matter how small, recoiled in horror, turned around, and started to run. As they hurried to reach the next house, I hollered loudly into the night, "Happy Halloween."

I know my parents wanted me to be as normal as possible, and to get to celebrate Halloween, but in retrospect, I know that our house put the horror into Halloween that year. The only thing worse would have been if we had given them candy and then made our announcement. I try not to think about it.

But I do remember my father saying, "Well, perhaps it's time to go into the kitchen and have a piece of that cake your grandmother made."

We were still at the table, when my mother got back from the hospital. She was smiling as she sat down. She patted my father's hand and said, "The doctors said the fever has broken, his lungs are good, and he can move his legs." She had tears in her eyes.

"It's going to be all right," she said. As I finished my cake, I knew that this time she meant it.

There Goes The Neighborhood

Visitors.

It was summer, it was hot, and I didn't want to be where I was, in the kitchen with only a squeaky fan for company. However, I had fiddled around for too long. My assignment was due.

This was the day when I had to create a realistic replica of a Roman temple to present to my Bible school class. I should have built the temple in stages, but forget that. I'd realized my mistake as I sat prepping and gluing tube-shaped Playtex® girdle boxes to the top of an upside-down cat-litter box. I'd been working for hours. The idea had been a good one, but the process for completing it had become far more involved than I'd imagined. Everything was taking far too long.

I'd had to cover the pictures of the half naked women that appeared on the Playtex® tubes with thick white paper to make them look like Roman columns. While the columns did look real as I began gluing them to the top of the cat box, I was running out of time. To make matters worse, I suddenly realized that I'd spilled glue. Two of the girdle columns were stuck, held firmly in place on the tabletop by white splotches of Elmer's glue. "What can happen next?" I asked myself? I didn't have to wait long for the answer.

The back doorbell rang, and I could see our neighbor from across the street, Mr. Rizzo, standing there in his sleeveless undershirt and gray sharkskin pants. A long strand of black oily hair had become dislodged from his never-a-hair-out-of-place pompadour, and he had his face pressed against the screen to see inside. He held an unlit cigar in one hand along with a white handkerchief. He leaned back, wiped his brow, and knocked again, harder. As he did I caught a glint of light from the big diamond ring he wore on his pinky finger. He usually wore a suit jacket too. I'd never seen him in any part of his underwear. I ran to open the door.

"Hi, Mr. Rizzo. Come on in," I said. "I'm just doing my . . ." I began to tell him about the temple, but he interrupted me.

"Hey, sweetie. How are you? Is your dad here?" His words came quickly and ran together. He often called me "sweetie," but usually he took time to talk to me and ask me what I was doing before he asked for one of my parents.

"I think he's in the back yard."

"Will you get him for me, sweetie," he asked, as he walked into the kitchen and looked back at his house through the kitchen window.

"Sure," I said, as I raced around the house to find my father. I liked Mr. Rizzo. He fixed my brother and me milkshakes at the soda fountain in his basement. The soda fountain was the only one I'd ever seen in a house. "You kids can have whatever you want when you come over here," Mr. Rizzo would say, waving his arm from one corner of the soda fountain to the other to show us that there were no limits.

But today Mr. Rizzo was acting weird, and he was sweating. I hoped my father could help him.

There had always been rumors about Mr. Rizzo. Some kids' parents told them not to speak to Mr. Rizzo because they said he was a man with a past, a crook trying to get back on the straight and narrow. When I asked my dad about Mr. Rizzo, he said, "Sam's trying. He's our friend." I didn't know exactly what that meant, but I could see at the time that the man standing at the window wasn't the Mr. Rizzo I knew.

"How you doing, Sam?" my father asked when we got back into the house.

"Thanks, sweetie." Mr. Rizzo looked at me as he grabbed my father by the elbow and took him into the dining room. "I've got to talk to your daddy now."

My part of the conversation was over. I went back to the kitchen table and started to work on the glue and the columns with a kitchen knife. I could still hear voices and tried not to listen right up until the time I heard Mr. Rizzo say, in a shaky voice, "They're going to break my legs." I dropped my knife.

"Shhh," my father said, but I could still hear. "You can go downstairs, go right now, go behind the furnace. There's a chair there. That's where Dena goes to smoke cigarettes when she gets mad. But, Sam, you'll have to promise me. You have to stay there, you can't come upstairs, you have to stay there until I tell you it's okay and I to come to get you."

"Yeah, thanks, Bob. I'll do what you say. I'm sorry . . ." but the voices trailed off as they came back into the kitchen.

"Mr. Rizzo's going to stay with us for awhile," my father said. "If anyone comes to the door, don't answer it until you come to get me. Do you understand? I'm the only one that will be opening the door until I tell you otherwise." I nodded. This scene was getting weirder than the girdle boxes and the temple.

"O.K.," I said. " I'll stay right here and clean up."

"Get downstairs, Sam," my father said, as he looked out the kitchen window. "There's a car pulling up in front of your house."

"Oh, my God," Mr Rizzo said, as he ran down the steps to the basement. It was then that I noticed he was still wearing his bedroom slippers.

"Just be quiet and don't say anything" my father said. "Don't go outside either. Just stay close until I tell you otherwise. Okay?"

"I'm scared," I said. I couldn't help it. "I heard Mr. Rizzo say . . ."

"Shhh," my father said. "There are some people coming to our door. Just don't say anything and whatever you do don't start crying. Just clean up that mess. This will all be over in a little while. Listen to what I say, and if you need to, agree with it."

The back doorbell rang. It was a sure sign of unknown company. My father went to the door and opened it.

"Hello," my father said and smiled. "Can I help you?"

"Yeah," a man's voice replied. "Do you know Sam Rizzo?"

"Yes, I know Sam," my father replied. "He's our neighbor. He lives across the street there." My father pointed to Rizzo's house. "Is everything all right?" he asked.

"Yeah, well, we're looking for Sam Rizzo. We're friends of his, just coming through town and wanted to see him. So, you must know him pretty well, being a neighbor." There was question in his voice.

"Oh yes," my father said, never missing a beat. "Sam developed this neighborhood and sold us this house. He and his wife, Phyllis, were the first people we met in town."

"Well, then," another voice said. "You must know where he is, probably know where we can find him."

"Oh, you're right," my father replied, still using his friendly voice. "I'd usually know what Sam's up to, but I just got back to town myself. I travel for a living, Monday through Friday, but when I got home this week, my wife said the Rizzos weren't home. They often go on trips, but my wife didn't say where this time."

"Is she home?" the other voice chimed in again. "Could she tell us when we might get to see him?"

"No," my father said. "She's not home either. She's gone to visit her sister, and I don't expect her back today."

"Well, that's too bad," the first man said. "We'd really hoped to see Sam, and I actually thought he might be expecting us."

"That's funny," my dad said. "It's not like Sam to leave if he's expecting company. There must have been a mix up. Tell you what. Do you have a card? If you'd like, when I see the lights come back on, I'll go over and tell Sam you were here and give him your card, or if you want to tell me your names..."

My father rattled on, but the first man interrupted him. "No, no, that won't be necessary. We'll just come back another time."

"Did you tell me what your names are?" my father asked. "My name's Bob." But I could hear the men walking away.

"No, we didn't tell you," the other man said. "It's all right. If you see Sam just tell him we'll be back. He'll know."

"Well, have a nice trip," my father called after them as he closed the door, looked my direction and winked at me.

The room filled with sounds of fans whirring throughout the house, and tears began to stream down my face. My father sighed, said, "Whew," and went downstairs.

I looked out the kitchen window as the two men got back into their car and lit cigarettes. I could hear my father whispering downstairs and walked down the steps until I could hear the conversation.

"No, Sam, this isn't it. You can't go yet. Those guys aren't going anywhere. They're waiting, and they'll be here long after dark. You're going to have to stay here until they really believe you're gone. When they've gone, you'll have just enough time to go home, get your bag, and head out of town. You'll have to get this thing cleaned up before you come back. In the meantime, I don't want you to tell any of us where you'll be, just call if you need anything and we'll take care of the house like usual. I'm assuming you sent Phyllis on ahead."

Mr. Rizzo must have nodded because Dad came upstairs and got a glass of water at the kitchen sink. "It's a good thing that Tim and Mom really are at your aunt's," he said. "It'll give you more time to clean up that mess. The temple probably will look good when you get the top on it." He rubbed my head and went into the dining room. He sat at the table for a long time, drumming his fingers and looking at the tablecloth.

I cleaned up the table and made a roof for the temple out of shirt-back cardboard that had come from the laundry. All this took a long time, and I didn't finish until after dinner. When I took my dishes to the sink, the men were still sitting in the car in front of the Rizzos' house.

I couldn't interest my father in dinner, but I took a plate down to Mr. Rizzo. I set up a tray table and remembered the napkins. After dinner, I tried to get Mr. Rizzo to play checkers like we did on other nights. He didn't want to so I offered to play Crazy Eights. I hated Crazy Eights, but he liked it.

He ruffled my hair and reached over to hug me. "I can't play anything right now," he said. His eyes were sad, and I looked teary. "But, you're the best," he repeated. "You're the very best, and when we can get back across the street, I'm going to fix you the biggest milkshake you've ever seen. It'll even have two cherries on the top."

He reached into his pocket, took out his handkerchief and blew his nose. He sat back in his chair. "Friends and family mean everything," he said. "That's what's important. Don't fall for anything else." Then he didn't say any more.

In the middle of the night, I heard noise in the basement. My father and Sam were hurrying upstairs.

"You're the best," I heard Mr. Rizzo say to my dad. "You're the very best."

The next day, when my mother and brother returned home, my mother asked what had happened. My father, who was sitting at the kitchen table, reading his paper answered, "The Rizzos decided to go on a trip. We're supposed to pick up the papers and the mail for a few days."

"Well, they're always going somewhere." my mother said. Looking at me, she asked, "Did you get the temple done? How did the girdle tubes do?"

"Oh, everything turned out all right, I guess. No one could tell the columns were girdle tubes. I knocked the roof off when I tripped and dropped the temple in the parking lot. Mrs. Wright told me not to get discouraged, but I don't think Bible school is for me."

"Oh, honey," my mother said in her "what can I say" mother's voice.

The newspaper rustled, and I heard my father's voice. "I've got it on good authority," he said, "that you're not impaired in any way. In fact from what I've heard you're the best, the very best."

He put down the paper for a second and winked at me. I don't remember if I winked back, but in the years that followed, I do remember having more milkshakes in Mr. Rizzo's basement. From that point on, the shakes always came with two cherries. As for Bible school, I did not return the next year or the next. I never returned.

The Christmas Pageant

Oh holy cow night.

* ✳ *

When the principal, the teachers, and the officers of the Elmwood School PTA gathered each year to place the large cardboard replica of Santa and his reindeer on the roof of the school, every kid knew that Christmas had finally come to town. Things were about to happen. We knew that beginning the next Monday morning, the call would go forth, and plans for the school Christmas pageant would capture the imagination of each and every child. During this short season, we knew each of us would have the chance to become a star.

As everyone watched Prancer, Dancer, and Rudolph ascend the ladder, there was speculation about whether or not school would have to be closed if Mr. Roley, our principal, fell off the roof. There also was adult dialogue about whether the Santa figure should be placed in front of the sleigh or where he would look like he was sitting inside. However, not one of the sleigh conversations was as important to those of us who were in the sixth grade as the one we were having about who would get the lead parts in the Christmas pageant.

Sixth grade was the year, the year for leading the rest of the school in the pledge of allegiance during school assemblies and for getting the lead parts in the Christmas pageant.

Because there was nothing to rival the excitement of the Christmas pageant, we all knew this was the time to crown our elementary school careers with important parts in the pageant, knowing for certain that those who became Mary and Joseph would be blessed with success for life.

My friend Darla, who also was Mr. Roley's daughter, said she thought I would be Mary, and I assured her that she would be. To my knowledge, there had never been a Mary who had worn glasses, and that didn't bode well for me. However, Darla was a good friend, and I was prepared for her to be Mary even though my father told me she sang through her nose.

My friend Donald said that Steven Stein would certainly be Joseph. He was Jewish and looked the part, so all the other boys would have to decide whether to try out to be shepherds or wise men.

Just then there was a cry from the top of the roof. "Look here, everyone. Boys and girls!"

Mr. Roley was calling down to us. "We're about to light Rudolph's nose to signal the beginning of the Christmas Season at Elmwood School."

The group looked up until the small red glow appeared. Everyone said "Aaah" in unison, as pageant season formally began.

"That's it," Mr.Roley said. "Tomorrow, you'll all get a chance to sign up to try out for parts in the Christmas pageant. And remember," he continued. "You parents still have a chance to sign up for costumes or refreshments. Just see Mrs. Harvey before you go home this evening. Thanks everyone and good night."

As we walked home, my mother assured me that she would not be signing up for the costume committee. She'd sell tickets, but she didn't want *anything* to do with anything involving cooking, and added she especially was not prepared to sew. "Just remember to tell them your mother's already signed up for something else."

I was barely paying attention. Since first grade, I'd done all the things I'd had to do to get in the position of getting a good part in the pageant, but did I dare to hope? Could a curly-haired girl with glasses be Mary? For just a moment, I imagined the baby Jesus and a solo.

On Monday morning, right after we said the pledge of allegiance and Steve Stein read the Bible story about no room at the inn, Miss Prunty told our class about this year's pageant. Each year there were different scenes, but we barely listened to those. When you were in sixth grade, you knew there was no point in doing the *Nutcracker Suite* scene or the scene about *Frosty the Snowman* unless you had to. Those parts were left to the little kids or to those who could not make THE most important scene, the Nativity in all its imagined glory.

Everyone knew it was better, in sixth grade, to be one of the shepherd's sheep than it was to settle for one of the parts that meant being with the little kids. So we waited until the moment she described this year's Nativity scene. As usual, this scene would be last, expressing the true spirit of Christmas. We would do the traditional story, with narration, and the solos would be sung by Mary, the wise men, and one of the shepherds. For no apparent reason other than that Miss Prunty said so, the *Little Drummer Boy* would wind things up at the end. Of course, there also were instructions that the narrator would have to speak the words of the Christmas story as they were told in the Bible's Revised Standard Version.

Miss Prunty gave us forms including our role descriptions, costume specifications, and tryout times. It was hard to focus on geography or anything else after her presentation, but because it was Christmas time, we looked to find Bethlehem on the map before we did our morning math.

The weeks that followed were busy ones. In art class, we made scenery for the pageant. In music class, we practiced carols and songs from the pageant. In math class, we figured out the current value of frankincense and myrrh. Of course, in the tryouts, as expected, Darla and Steve Stein won.

The rest of us were assigned roles. I was asked to be narrator on the basis that they thought I could memorize the whole story. Donald had to be a shepherd, but they changed his role when, in rehearsal, he dropped raisins from the behind of the stuffed sheep he was carrying. I thought he'd earned his spot as the third wise man.

I didn't mind being narrator much. After endless hours of boring my father, I got the whole part memorized. I was asked to stand at the side of the stage dressed in a traditional choir robe that was made from of a square white table cloth. The only thing Mother needed to do to make the robe was to cut a diamond-shaped hole in its center for my head. The whole family was proud when she was able to make my costume after all.

On the night of the pageant, Darla wore the flowing blue and white robes of Mary. She did sing through her nose and almost dropped the baby Jesus when she tried to hit the high note in "O, Holy Night." Other than that, things went pretty much as planned for the sixth grade. By performance night, everybody in the sixth grade knew that the Christmas pageant would not take anyone to Hollywood. When the *Little Drummer Boy* appeared, even Debbie knew she would not be a star, not even for that evening.

As Eric Bowman walked down the aisle and approached the crèche, he beat the big bass drum attached to his chest proudly. Smiling broadly, he was blissfully unaware that the fly on his pants was completely open. Each step caused all the mothers along the aisles to hide their eyes, fearful of yet another surprise.

Eric didn't know anything about his fly until Steve Stein told him when he arrived at the crèche. Red with embarrassment, Eric stood in stark contrast to the other only white faces of the crèche scene. The spotlights faded to black, to the applause of our parents and friends. I was pleased; I'd only muffed three lines.

Eric Bowman didn't come back to school until Christmas vacation was over.

Word was he had contracted a serious case of embarrassment.

The Gambler

Stuff that dreams are made of.

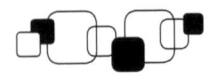

*"There was a place with wide, palm-lined avenues
and casinos on either side where people
bet on wheels, cards, dice, which made them feel
alive and what they thought was happy."*
—Mark Irwin

Mr. Rizzo told me that Las Vegas was the town where people bet to make their dreams come true. He said that Reno was the place where people bet to try and pay for their dreams that had gone bad.

He tried to explain the difference to me as we sat on the top step of his front porch on a very hot day in August. I'd seen him through our kitchen window as he walked through his front door carrying a newspaper in one hand and an unlit cigar in the other. He wasn't dressed neatly, as he usually was. Instead, he was wearing a wrinkled pair of brown sharkskin pants, and one of the white, sleeveless tee-shirts that tough guys like Marlon Brando wore in the movies. He was wearing his bedroom slippers with no socks, and his hair was hanging over his eyes as if he hadn't combed it in days.

I knew Mrs. Rizzo said he'd been gone "on business," but he'd been gone for two months. She said he'd been to

Vegas, a place I'd seen on TV. At sixteen, Vegas looked interesting to me, a place I pictured with palm trees, neon lights, and girls dressed mostly in feathers. However, my mother had described it as being "sin city," while my father simply said it was "hotter than hell." I couldn't imagine it was any hotter than it was in Ohio in August, but when I saw Mr. Rizzo walk outside, I decided I'd say "hello" and get some answers for myself.

As I walked out of our house, Mr. Rizzo didn't seem to notice. He kept his eyes on his paper and chewed his cigar, but he didn't look up as he usually did whenever our back door slammed. I hollered at him as I began to walk across the street.

"Welcome home, Mr. Rizzo," I said. This time, he raised his head, but when he smiled at me and said, "Thanks, honey," his voice seemed weak and his smile was a small one. He closed the paper, folded it, and put it down beside him. Without getting up, he motioned for me to come over and sit down.

As I reached the steps, I said. "Boy, I'll bet you're tired. I understand it's a long trip from Las Vegas."

"It certainly is," he replied, "a very long way from Las Vegas to this neighborhood." He repeated my words in his quiet voice.

"Well, we're glad to have you home," I said in a happy voice, thinking that enthusiasm would cheer him up. He nodded, and when I got closer and sat down next to him, I could see he hadn't shaved.

"You must really be tired," I continued, but the words came out as a question.

"Oh, I'm sorry, honey," he said slowly. "I've just got some things on my mind, but how are you?"

"Oh, I'm fine," I answered as I looked at his shirt. It was ribbed, like an undershirt. It was an undershirt. Mr. Rizzo, our best-dressed neighbor was sitting on his front porch in his undershirt. The scene looked like something out of New York City, where people sit on their front porches in their undershirts in the middle of summer, where your imagination can almost smell the heat and garbage, and where you wait for firemen to open a fire hydrant to clean and cool the streets. But this was Ohio, where everything was the same—clipped lawns and newly paved sidewalks. Only the newly planted small trees wilted in the heat, and nothing ever smelled worse than barbeque. What was Mr. Rizzo thinking? Why didn't he just put on some shorts and get a beer?

"I know Gary missed you," I continued to try and make a positive connection. "He seemed to enjoy Bible School. I heard him practicing a song for the pageant. He had a solo, you know." I kept going, and Mr. Rizzo nodded in agreement and worked on smiling at me when he thought I expected him to.

"Yes, he's growing. He's getting to be a big boy. He's too big for some things, too small for others, I guess." He was talking, but I thought he was talking to himself. "I wish he'd sing less, and play more ball. He's got to toughen up some..." He stopped suddenly as if I were overhearing something he hadn't meant to say.

"Well, you have to be ten here before you ever get any serious consideration for Little League." I jumped right in, trying to sound grown up, trying to have him think this was a normal conversation. He nodded again, looked down at his feet, and shrugged his shoulders. I glanced at his feet too, but I didn't notice anything unusual.

"Well, tell me about Las Vegas. Will you? I've just gotten so many stories, and you're the only person I know who's really been there." He lifted his head and looked straight ahead at the street.

There wasn't anything or anyone in the street to look at, but this is when he said, "Las Vegas is a place where people go to make their dreams come true." Then he stopped and looked at me. "That's why I went there," he said. "I had some dreams I wanted to come true." He looked back toward the street, but he looked like he was thinking about another place.

"When I wanted to build this neighborhood," he said, "I went to Las Vegas. It was a lucky place for me, and this neighborhood was the result. I never thought I'd have to go back." He was saying more than he meant to say again. I could tell because his voice got softer and softer, almost like he didn't want to hear, but he didn't stop talking.

"Now, there will be other trips to places like Toledo, to Cleveland, maybe even to Reno." He stopped, looked at me, then looked down at his hands. I could tell that he didn't expect me to reply. I looked at his hands too. His diamond pinky ring was missing from the little finger on his left hand. I'd never seen him without it, but he still wore a diamond horseshoe ring on his right ring finger. He twisted the ring as though he were going to take it off. However, he just kept twisting it around and around on his finger.

He looked directly at me, and in more of his regular voice, he said, "We'll see how lucky I get. Las Vegas has lots of palm trees. It's the jewel of the desert, but it's also a place where your dreams can be put on hold." He winked, smiled at me and said. "But it's not the only place. Some dreams just take more time. I remember the time when . . . "

He went on to tell me about how people didn't believe him, when he, Sam Rizzo, said he'd go into construction, how people found out that he built the best houses in town, how there were lots more to be built if you could only . . . " He kept going, and then he told me about when he'd met my father.

I kept nodding and smiling, knowing Mr. Rizzo didn't want me to say a thing, not knowing why he was telling me these stories or what they had to do with my question about Las Vegas.

"Well, I'm glad you're back." It finally was time for me to say something. "Sorry it's so hot! Can you believe this heat?" We both looked out at the street. The air looked wavy as I looked toward our house.

"Hot," Mr. Rizzo laughed. "This is nothing. Las Vegas is hotter than hell. Oh," he stumbled, "I'm sorry, but it's in the desert, you know."

So far, I couldn't tell why anyone would want to go there. "I hope you get to stay home for awhile," I answered. "We miss you when you're gone."

He looked right at me and smiled. I thought I'd pleased him.

"Thanks, honey. You don't have to worry about me going back to Vegas. I'm done there. Now, I hope I'll only have to go as far as Cleveland to get things lined up. Otherwise, I'll have to go to Reno. It's in Nevada too, but it's not like Vegas."

"Is it a place that I'd like better?" I asked. "Vegas doesn't sound that great with the heat and all . . ." I would have gone on, but Mr. Rizzo interrupted me.

"No," Mr. Rizzo said. "Reno isn't a great place either. It's the end of the road for people like me. It's where you get to pay for your bad dreams, for the dreams that don't come true." He was looking off into the distance as though I wasn't there. He reached over and picked up his newspaper, threw his chewed cigar into the bushes, looked at me, smiled, and said. "It's time for me to go inside. Thanks for coming over. I'll see you again real soon."

I was too old for him to tousle my hair as he'd done for years. He simply patted my knee, got up and went into the house. He didn't wait for me to leave.

As I walked back across the street, I felt sad without knowing exactly why. Mr. Rizzo looked and acted so differently. I knew I hadn't done anything, but Mr. Rizzo had not been happy to see me. I knew he'd been trying not to hurt my feelings.

When I got home, I ate two double chocolate Little Debbie snack cakes with a big glass of real lemonade, but even they didn't help. My conversation with Mr. Rizzo had put me in a sad mood. I went into my bedroom, moved my desk fan to a place where it could blow directly into my face, and opened my diary. I wrote an entry that said: "I will never go to Reno, let alone Las Vegas." I also noted I wouldn't go to any other place that I thought would make me as sad as Mr. Rizzo was as he sat on his front porch on that hot day in August.

In the coming months, I saw Mr. Rizzo in variations of the same undershirt outfit, sitting on his front porch. He didn't always read the paper. Sometimes, he'd just smoke a cigar and look off into space. Often, he put his head down, cupped both hands and drew them over his head to push the hair back from his eyes. Sometimes, he sat with his head in his hands as if what he was thinking about was too heavy for his shoulders to carry.

Several times, when I'd go out onto the front porch to cool off, I'd see the red tip of his cigar in the night. He never called over like he had in the past. In fact, he didn't say much of anything to me from then on. While he smiled and waved from time to time, he never asked me to come over and he stopped coming to our house altogether.

Things had changed. Even my father, who still went to visit Mr. Rizzo even when he wasn't invited, couldn't get him to cheer up. All Dad ever told us was that we should wave at Mr. Rizzo and try to talk to him. Dad said he was sure we cheered Mr. Rizzo up even though we couldn't tell.

"We're going to be good friends to him," was all my dad said when I asked what was going on. Later, I found Mr. Rizzo had run out of money. The money that he'd kept in his freezer wrapped in butcher paper, marked as T-bone steaks or rump roasts, had been paid to the men in Toledo who ran backroom card games. Mr. Rizzo needed to find another jackpot.

It didn't take long for Mr. Rizzo to be gone almost all the time. When I'd ask Mrs. Rizzo about him, she'd say he was in Toledo, then more often in Cleveland. Finally, she said he needed to go to Reno. She said she thought he'd be there for a long time.

I remembered his words about Reno and worried. I wondered what dreams had gone bad, what he'd had to pay for. I hoped he could hit his jackpot before his business associates in Toledo and Cleveland found him.

Things changed across the street. Gary and Mrs. Rizzo got used to living by themselves. In time, Arnie Newton, Mrs. Rizzo's old boss from the Oldsmobile garage, gave her his wife's old gray cutlass. She used it to drive to her new job at the Reformed Alliance church.

Gary remained a solitary figure. When his pal Pammy Bosch got old enough to have a boyfriend, he pretty much stayed at home by himself. My brother and I worried about him. From time to time, we invited him over for a game of gin rummy or cribbage, but Mrs. Rizzo wouldn't allow it. When my mother asked why, she said, "There'll be no more cards, dice, or bets of any kind for my son."

In time, there weren't any more stories or gossip about the Rizzos. While everyone still wondered what would happen to Gary, no one said much. There just wasn't much more to say. The neighborhood became mired in middle age, with more interesting developments growing up around it.

When I graduated from high school, the streets that had all been one or two blocks long extended for several blocks in each direction. When I came back one year for summer vacation, I told my father I could hardly recognize the neighborhood.

"What you see here was Sam Rizzo's dream. Too bad," Dad said and shook his head.

Within a month of that conversation there was news from Reno. Sam Rizzo had died in his room in Reno's brand-new Motel Six. He'd become a low-dollar dealer at Harrah's. When he missed two shifts at work, the pit boss called the motel. The manager said they found Sam lying on his bed with the TV on. "Everything looked normal," the manager said. He looked like he'd just gone to sleep.

On the nightstand at his bedside, they found a half-eaten beef Hungry-Man® dinner, a half full bottle of Miller High Life, and a roll of five hundred one dollar bills held together with a rubber band. There were no other personal effects.

Sam's obituary listed him as a local "developer." My father said Sam would have been pleased. "Sam liked to say he built a street of dreams. In our case, I think he did."

Honeysuckle

Honeysuckle in bloom.

My father often told me that it was best to fill in all the blanks on a questionnaire, test, or application. His words: "Blank spaces indicate doubt, insecurity. Don't look blank either," he continued. "Be sure to nod, smile, or in some way indicate that you're involved in the conversation. Be there. Show up. Take a risk. Nothing begets nothing. Don't live life as though you have nothing to offer. Remember, there's always a good chance you're going to get something right."

He also followed his own advice when it came to answering questions from his children.

"What kind of bush is that, Dad?" I was nine at the time, pointing to a yellow bush that our neighbor was planting in his front yard.

"Honeysuckle," Dad answered. "That's a honeysuckle bush. It only blooms in the spring."

End of discussion, the answer was complete. Until I was thirty years old, I believed those pretty yellow bushes were honeysuckle. I believed that right up to the time I ordered some honeysuckle bushes for our new house, up to the time when I told the nurseryman that the bushes he was delivering weren't "honeysuckle" bushes.

I puzzled out loud. "Honeysuckle bushes are the ones with the pretty yellow flowers aren't they?"

"No," the nursery guy said. "No such thing as honeysuckle bushes with bright yellow flowers. I think you must be wanting forsythia bushes. What you're asking for sounds like forsythia." He went to his truck and got a catalog.

"Look here. Is this what you want?" He pointed to a picture of a perfectly lovely honeysuckle bush.

"Yup. That's it, a beautiful honeysuckle-forsythia bush. That's the one, the one I've been sure is honeysuckle." He got back in his truck and delivered forsythia bushes two days later.

Shortly after this embarrassing incident, I had occasion to ask my father about the honeysuckle bush. I shared my recollection of my youthful conversation with him.

"Forsythia, eh?" He often cocked an eyebrow when he was trying to think of an answer. And he often answered a question with a question when he didn't have a plausible answer.

"Well, you asked. I might not have known about forsythia, but you wanted an answer, and I gave you one. I'm pretty sure I thought it was honeysuckle then—I don't lie on purpose, you know, but you wanted an answer, and I gave you the best one I had at the time."

"Now it's my turn," he continued. "I have a question. Do both forsythia and honeysuckle bloom in the spring?"

"Yes," I replied.

"So even then, part of my answer was right?" It was my turn to cock an eyebrow.

"See?" he said. "Goes to show you—there's always a chance you'll get something right. And you got some right back then and the rest right eventually—right?"

This time I cocked my whole head. "What?" I heard the tone of astonishment in my voice.

"Yeah. No harm done and another lesson learned."

"You're not serious." I couldn't believe he was still talking.

"No, really. Now you know the bonus lesson."

I shrugged, speechless.

"Always consider the source. You've heard that before—that's something you need to remember too. Always consider the source."

Yet another example of parenting by cliché. I was stunned. He finally was done.

He shook his head, laughing as he left the room. "I'm funny," he said. "I'm just too damn funny."

Going Home

Aids comes to town.

*A*IDS arrived in our neighborhood in a green Pontiac Firebird. My mother reported that a bright green car with a bird decal on its hood came screeching around the corner of Central Boulevard. It made enough noise to get her to the kitchen window, where she saw our old neighbor Gary Rizzo struggle to get out of the front seat of his car. Gary was still in his twenties but had left town years before. For his return, Mother said, he was dressed in a high-fashion leather suit, but she also said he walked slowly, like an old man, when he walked toward the front door of his childhood home. He reached for the railing to assist him in taking the two steps to the porch. Mother said he hesitated before ringing the doorbell to call his mother to the door.

"It must have been a big surprise for Phyllis," Mother said. "I could tell by the way she reached for her face and threw back her head when she saw him. After that, she pulled his arms toward her, hugged him, and closed the door. That was all I saw, but the whole thing seemed weird. Gary driving that loud bird car and parking in front of the house instead of in the driveway. Why would he go in the front door? I'd only seen him use that door one time, long ago, on a Prom night. Even though I could see it was Gary, he didn't look anything like the Gary we knew."

This news came via one of my mothers regular phone calls. Ever since I'd left Central Boulevard, years before, mother made it a practice to call me every Sunday to bring me back home with news of the neighborhood. But this was different. On this day, there were more questions than stories or explanations. Mother was in the midst of a mystery, and Phyllis Rizzo was not calling to fill her in on any of the details.

Since Gary Rizzo made his first entrance into the neighborhood in a salmon and white convertible decades earlier, he had become a major source of neighborhood interest, as the Rizzos continued their over-the-top ways. With a child in the house, the soda fountain, velvet sofas, and velvet paintings were featured less. Instead, everything was adapted to the needs and whims of the beautiful little dark-skinned boy, who seldom played outside but who often could be seen inside the house, pressing his nose and hands firmly against the glass of the Rizzo's large front bay window.

Every year, there were birthday parties that included pony rides, clowns, and real cotton-candy makers. There were stacks of hot dogs on dog-shaped platters along with a mountain-shaped fountain of Coca-Cola® that really worked. In the middle of it all, Gary always stood alone, dressed in some type of flamboyant birthday outfit. One year, he was dressed as a matador, the next year as a dinosaur with a spiked tail, and yet another as an Emmett Kelly clown. But each year, the only thing that was real were his tears. Even in the midst of such wonderful events, someone hurt Gary's feelings, and the party ended quickly, with the dispersal of elaborate party favors. When the parties were over, Gary remained where he was, at Two Central Boulevard, with only his mother and father as his most favored companions.

"He's too good looking," my mother said. "Kids are envious. He has everything and he's gorgeous to boot. Just think about it. He's prettier than most girls. Most girls would love to have beautiful black hair like that and eyelashes that are as long as most people's fingernails. His eyes are browner than Bambi's and his skin almost glows. He looks almost perfect, is dressed perfectly, and has too perfect a life for most people to accept."

Most kids never accepted Gary any more than their parents had accepted Mr. and Mrs. Rizzo. Although kids never refused invitations to Gary's parties, they didn't feel it necessary to invite him in return. For most of his growing years, Gary lived with his advantages, having only an occasional girl friend, who was only a friend, visit him at his house. However, he did feel comfortable with our family and often came across the street to visit when my brother and I returned home for the holidays.

Gary's interests lay elsewhere. He turned out to be a good student. He liked the company of books and often wrote to me at college to see if I had suggestions for things to read. In his letters, he referred to books, but he also made note of petty slights and increasing annoyance with his parents. He credited himself with being intellectually gifted, complaining often about being at a loss for suitable company. With each letter, his criticisms became more pointed, nastier, and more negative. Nothing pleased him as much as he pleased himself.

In answering his letters, I did so without comment, making only reading suggestions that could be described as uplifting. As a result, his letters became more argumentative. Then they stopped all together. Although he still came to see me when I returned home, we stopped our conversations about ideas and attitudes, even as I noticed the changes in his dress and manner that suggested an increasing sense of unease. However, he still looked great, wonderful, almost perfect.

I recounted much of this as my mother continued to worry and wonder on the phone. Gary's returning home in a bird-decorated Firebird was far bigger news than his leaving.

As mother continued, I recalled the last time I visited with Gary. Having finished graduate school, I was on a brief trip home before moving to Chicago. Gary had just finished college, even though he hadn't graduated, and had walked across the street to tell me he was moving too.

As he walked across the street, I noted he was walking with an easier gait. Not surprisingly, he was perfectly dressed in starched khaki pants and a pink, pony-decorated button-down shirt. His hair was cut very short, but he wore something I had never seen before, a large diamond earring in his left ear. He was a stunning figure as he reached out to hug me.

My initial reaction was to be impressed. Bad things had happened to the Rizzos since I'd last seen Gary. Mr. Rizzo had gone to Reno, Nevada, to try and make up for his financial reverses by becoming a dealer at Harrah's®. He died in a nearby motel, alone, with a roll of five hundred one-dollar bills in his pocket.

When Sam died, Mrs. Rizzo had gone back to work at the Buick garage as a receptionist. This time, she wasn't asked to sit on the hoods of any cars as an attractive hood ornament. This time, she sat at the switchboard behind the cashier's table. This time, her job depended on getting the messages right. She also joined the Holy Alliance Free Church to create new prospects among the aging parishioners. As a result, she marginally lifted her spirits as she created barely enough income to keep her house. There were no more new cars or parties, just the house and bills on the kitchen table.

Considering the changes, I thought Gary looked remarkably well.

"I've come to say good-bye," he said, "and to give you this." He handed me a small leatherette-bound book of Shakespeare love sonnets. "Thanks for helping me to like such things."

Then he started a litany of complaints. The town was too small, too dumb. His mother was too old, too dumb, and pretty well washed up. His father had been an embarrassment. He was meant for better things.

"I've met people from Houston," he said, with a note of awe in his voice. "You'd love them. They read; they're smart; they're absolutely beautiful. Some of them even have their pictures in the Houston magazines. My very best friend even gave me this earring. What do you think? I don't know many girls who have an engagement ring this big. Do you?"

I admitted I didn't know about the engagement rings, but in that moment, with Gary gesturing and smiling in a curiously seductive way, I began to understand what was in Houston and why he was choosing to go there.

"I hope you'll be happy," I said when he got up to go. "I hope that you find what you're looking for. I hope you enjoy your friends."

"Oh, I will," he said, winking at me. "If you're ever in Houston, come and visit. You're one of the few people from here who will understand what I'm doing there."

I nodded and briefly hugged him good-bye. He walked back across the street, the one he'd crossed so many times as a child, the street he wanted to leave behind, the one that he hoped would never require his return.

My mother's voice brought me back. "He was walking like a little old man. Are you listening? And, that car. Where do you think he got a car like that. Phyllis says he's been waiting tables in Houston. Where do you suppose he got the money?"

Mother was not about to stop, so I interrupted. "Well, Mom, it will be interesting to hear what the story is. You keep me posted. I hope this is good news for Phyllis and not just another selfish Gary episode."

"I don't think you ever liked him," she said, "but I'll fill you in next Sunday."

The next Sunday in Colorado came with complications. Our Sunday school class at the time had one of those discussions about who should and who should not be saved, who deserved to be served by the people of God and who didn't. Much of the conversation had centered around the newest horror, the AIDS epidemic. When the phone rang, I was emotionally ill, saddened, and sickened by church-driven certainty, but I was happy for the break of my mother's call.

"You will not believe it!" she started. "The thing with Gary is really something. He's got cancer, black spots all over. I went over, and he looks like he's more than a hundred. He said something about it not being an ordinary cancer. Now, the people from the health department are coming around. They don't think people should be near him. They're thinking about putting a sign on Rizzo's house." She seemed puzzled.

"Your father says we shouldn't go over there until Gary leaves. He says we've got an obligation to you kids and your family not to expose ourselves to such a terrible thing. But I didn't know cancer was contagious, and Phyllis is just beside herself. She said she'd tell me later, but that there are things that are even worse. I can't imagine . . ."

I felt a big ball of something growing in my stomach. How could all these issues of the day be coming home to roost at my mother's house? I wanted to throw up. The nerve ball was expanding into my chest, but I could still talk.

139

"I think I know what's wrong with Gary, Mom. Even though he has cancer, it comes from having another disease. It's new to us, and it's awful. It's called AIDS, Mom. Gary probably is a homosexual, and he probably got it from having sex with other men."

"Oh, don't talk like that," she said. "I won't listen to you any more if you say such things. Cancer is enough. What you're saying is too much. He grew up here, right here in this neighborhood. Where would he even learn about such a thing? Poor Phyllis. I don't think I've even met one of those kinds of people before."

"Well, Mom. I think you know one now. What are you going to do?"

She cleared her throat, then made a little squeaking noise to try out her voice. "I guess I'll just have to find out what they need, unless you don't think it's safe to go there. If you really think there's a danger . . . What do you think?"

"I think you should do what is right for you, Mom. I think you should do what you'd ordinarily do. Remember, Mom, even when you were scared, you'd always tell me, don't let other people make you afraid."

"Hmm," she said. That's all she said. Several times I had to ask if she was still there. At last she cleared her throat again and said, "I'll just keep my hands in my pockets. If I don't touch anything, we'll probably all be fine. I'll just keep my hands in my pockets. I'll call later. In the meantime, say a prayer for Gary and Phyllis. You probably better say one for me too because now I'm going to tell your father what I've decided."

In the weeks and months that followed, my father remained annoyed by my mother's decision. Even though he didn't mind having Phyllis for dinner and sent books over for Gary to read, he never accepted AIDS into his neighborhood. While he never tried to stop my mother from crossing the street, he didn't cross it and didn't want to understand. My mother crossed the street every day to help Phyllis with the bills and to remind Gary he should be nice to his mother no matter how mad he was at God or the world.

The only time that I went home during the AIDS episode, I called Gary and asked if I could come to visit. I could hear him catch his breath before saying "please do." He quickly added. "You'll be my second visitor. In all the time I've been here, only your mother has come to see me. Now you'll be the second."

When I crossed the street, everything had changed. The Rizzo's house had been completely remodeled. There were no more stuffed animals, or gaudy slipcovers; everything was medicinal. Mrs. Rizzo's chair and TV were the only two items of furniture remaining. A wheelchair and a walker from better days had replaced the furniture. There were boxes of tubes and stainless steel pans and poles that had bags hanging from them.

Mrs. Rizzo motioned me toward Gary's room without any special greeting. The room had been the master bedroom, but now there was a sheet of plastic hanging over the door. As I moved through the opening in the plastic to step inside the bedroom, I knew I had entered the world of Gary's dying.

There, in the middle of the room, Gary lay on a hospital bed. Except for a metal folding chair placed by the bedside, there was no other furniture. Everything else involved medical instruments.

He turned to look at me, a single figure in what felt like an enormous space. Gary wasn't perfect any more. He was without his hair, without his eyelashes, without his clothing. His big beautiful brown "Bambi" eyes were expressionless, like the small flat buttons eyes of his old Teddy bears. What had been his glowing skin was parched and pulled back tightly against the shockingly skeletal bones of his face. A sheet was draped over his swollen stomach and lower body. He raised his hand in a half greeting. "Hi," he said quietly. His fingers seemed elongated in their silhouette. He reminded me of one of the alien beings in the movie *Close Encounters of the Third Kind*.

He looked directly at me, but he didn't smile. His look seemed to question me.

"I'm glad to be here with you, Gary." I paused. "But I don't think much of your outfit."

Thankfully, he smiled and replied, "Now, you'll just have to look for the beauty inside."

We both half laughed, but there weren't many more jokes that day. We had some bemused moments discussing the "best laid plans," but more often we simply sat together. He tired quickly but didn't seem in a hurry for me to go. "I'll stay until you fall asleep," I said. "And, I'll try not to put you to sleep as quickly as I usually can." Again, he smiled and I smiled too.

I reached over to hold his hand, but he said, "Please don't . . . just in case." AIDS was a new disease. "Let's be sure," he added. "I don't recommend this."

I sat back in my chair and left shortly after, when he drifted off into what looked to be a shallow sleep.

When I left the bedroom, I went into the kitchen to talk to Phyllis. My mother was there, and they were reviewing a pile of insurance claims. My mother was putting some things in piles and others in boxes for filing. As she worked,

I noticed she was wearing a pair of the white cotton gloves that she often wore to church.

Although I left the next day, AIDS stayed longer. Near the end, mother helped Phyllis find a large black woman named Olive to come and care for Gary. Olive bathed Gary and touched him without fear. To my knowledge, she was the first and only black person ever to be in the Rizzo's house.

At the end, Mother said, Olive told her and Mrs. Rizzo that death would be there that day. "How do you know?" my mother asked, but Olive simply said she knew. She told my mother not to go home until things were over. She gave my mother a tip. "Death comes from the feet, honey. So you'll know too, just when, it comes from the feet. Get ready when you see it." My mother told me that in an odd way Olive's words made things easier.

Death did come from the feet, mother said. That's when AIDS left the neighborhood, as three unlikely companions linked arms to bear witness. One of them kept her hands in her pockets.

The Lamp

The heirloom.

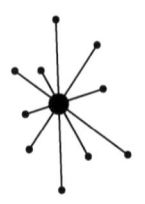

"A thing of beauty is a joy forever." That's what poet John Keats said, but in the end, or even in the beginning, who decides what is beautiful?

Not long ago, I sat in my living room looking at the "family treasure" my mother had passed along to me. She described this oddly constructed piece as a thing of beauty. Coming from my father's side of the family, this large antique lamp looks like two soccer balls stacked one upon the other, held together in a vertical line by the faux chimney piercing the middle of each sphere. Both globes are painted yellowish green, and they feature large, nondescript maroon flowers, reminiscent of oversized hibiscus, meandering around the circumference of each in an annoyingly consistent pattern.

In thinking of how to describe the lamp in an imagined eBay ad, I puzzled over the phrasing. Would "splashes of color" be an apt description of the design? Perhaps such an innocent phrase might draw interest when combined with other market-sensitive words such as "antique," "heirloom," "hand-painted," "original," and "one-of-a-kind."

Immediately upon receiving the lamp, I knew that my mother was right when she said that I might not appreciate its beauty right away. It might take time, but eventually I would come to love the family legacy that it represented.

She was right on the first count. I did not appreciate the gift, not for a minute. However, she was wrong on the second count. I never came to appreciate the gift and remain sure that "eventually" will never come. Even the lore that came with the lamp, as in the story, "It had provided the only source of dependable light that my grandparents shared when they were missionaries to the Indians," was not enough to stir any positive emotion.

However, the lamp remained. My negative feelings were not strong enough to overcome the real family legacy that the gift represented or the overwhelming sense of guilt that had been successfully passed along from generation to generation, allowing such an unfortunately odd lamp to occupy a place in the homes of at least four generations of our family.

The greater truth in the story emerged later. In a moment of weakness my mother admitted, "In the end, it really doesn't matter what you think of the lamp. It will break your father's heart if you break the chain. It's yours now. I had it for over thirty years. I got it this far. It's your turn now."

There was no doubt about my obligation. Guilt always hovers in the air whenever there's a prospect for finding that lamp another home. There's an evil sense of ancestry that dooms us all to living with things that others want to get out of their houses.

There's no need to question why something better had not come your way or to think about adopting a family with ancestors who had better taste. Just keep the damn thing, whatever it is, for at least twenty years, then pass it along. Make up your own family story—it doesn't even have to be a good one if you can impose an appropriate dose of guilt.

I know the lamp is not an isolated incident. Others have to deal with their own ugly icons. I've been in other homes that sported spotted ceramic rabbits made by dead relatives. What do you do with a dozen of those?

I've also eaten dinner in a home where dinner was formally served in a dark dining room that featured a painting of a large herd of cows grazing in a field with two trees and a small hill. Supposedly, the painting was a rare Copley, but I found the rarest part of the scene to be the cows who were painted with their rear ends facing the eating audience. It made me wonder which of the tow-headed children at the table would one day find this bucolic disaster darkening their door.

Aging relatives must believe that longevity allows them to become arbiters of the family legacy. While there's no accounting for taste, I've learned it's better to accept this inevitable fact than to taste the rage of a mother or father who just wants to pass the damn thing on.

When my mother and father left our house, leaving the legacy lamp behind, my father looked at me, pointed back toward the lamp and spoke. "It's beautiful. Take my word for it. No kidding. You'll get used to it, no problem. Really, believe it."

After looking at the lamp for years now, I take those recorded words as one of the few times my father lied to me without trying to make things better. Since that time, I've tried to adjust to its presence, but my mind has not changed. In an effort not to have to lie to my daughter, I've done the only thing I could think of to reduce the odds of having the legacy conversation.

I've moved the lamp to hazardous perches. I've placed it in harm's way. I've held the cat up to look at the light, moved its paw to mock a strike at the chimney. So far, nothing has happened, no big winds to blow it over, no clumsy visitors to strike it as they come down the stairs, no wildly rambunctious cat fights to take out the light.

As I wait here, aging, I continue to think of just the right words for eBay, dreaming of a person who admires the lamp, someone who might want to take it home, or for one big spring storm that will unfurl the curtains to knock the lamp off its table into shards of history.

Heirloom: An odd ancestral piece, kept at the behest of ancient relatives for the purpose of torturing those of their line to remember the questionable place their family has occupied in history, in a past uninspired by significant achievement or accomplishments of note.

Mink

The best gift ever.

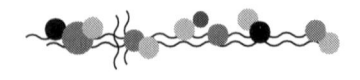

The box was big, rectangular, wrapped in a mass of pink shiny paper, and decorated with a crisscrossed piece of white gauzy ribbon that topped the box in a huge bow. Mr. Rizzo put his cigar back in his mouth and used both hands to grip the sides of the package to get it out of the back seat of his pink and white Oldsmobile convertible.

I was watching him walk into his house from across the street, from behind our kitchen window, where I was making myself a peanut butter sandwich for lunch. It was a beautiful fall day, and I had walked home for lunch to take a break from the Johnny Marzetti casserole that always appeared for lunch in the school cafeteria on Wednesdays. Now, the peanut-butter sandwich was even more appealing because I knew that the big pink box was something special, something that would be the source of neighborhood gossip, and something that I would know about first. I got closer to the window, hoping that Mr. Rizzo wouldn't be able to close the back door behind him, hoping I'd get to hear something to give me a clue about the contents of the box.

"Oh, Sam, honey!" I heard the words. "Oh, my God! I can't believe it! Oh, it's beautiful. This is unbelievable. I'm such a lucky girl!"

That was it. A silence followed that I didn't want to think about. I could see the back door close just as my mother pulled in the driveway.

"I'm home," I hollered through the window, knowing that my lunch-time visit was unexpected and that the open back door would scare her to death.

"Oh, thanks," Mom said. "What are you eating. Do you want some chips? Make sure to drink some milk with that."

She would have gone on and on, but I interrupted.

"Something big is up at the Rizzos' again," I noted, as I chewed my sandwich.

"Don't' talk with your mouth full. What are you talking about?" she asked.

I responded by chewing deliberately for a very long time before answering. "Mr. Rizzo just took a huge pink box into the house, and it must have been good because Mrs. Rizzo was talking so loudly I could hear her through the window. 'Oh, Sam, I'm such a lucky girl!'" I mimicked Mrs. Rizzo as I batted my eyelashes at my mother.

My mom laughed, but quickly caught herself. "Don't be disrespectful. It's Phyllis' birthday, and as you know, Sam likes to make a big deal. She probably got something wonderful again."

While I thought I heard a hint of envy in my mother's reply, I had to get back to school and couldn't explore that possibility.

"Well, it's your job to get information for me by the time I get home this afternoon. I've never seen such a big box. Maybe you should just call Phyllis and wish her a happy birthday." I rinsed my plate, finished the glass of milk that my mother had put in front of me during our conversation, and headed out the door. I was fourteen, and it was good to have the freedom to walk home for lunch and the almost adult status that allowed me to give my mother an idea about how to spend her afternoon.

"Have a good afternoon," Mom said, but I knew she was as curious about the big pink box as I was.

When I walked home in the afternoon, I enjoyed the color of the changing leaves and appreciated the Indian summer weather that made me sweat slightly as I approached our house. I couldn't wait to change into to my favorite madras Bermudas one more time before the cold of November changed my wardrobe to wool.

As I approached the house, I could hear voices in the kitchen. One was Mother's and the other was Mrs. Rizzo's. "Life is good, I thought. All things are about to be revealed."

As I came through the back door and went into the kitchen, my thoughts were translated into literal truth. There at the kitchen table in the 80°-plus weather were my mother and Mrs. Rizzo. Mother was wearing the same sleeveless blouse she'd had on at lunch, but Mrs. Rizzo was sitting there, without a drop of sweat, in a full-length fur coat.

"Hi, honey. It's mink," she said, looking down at her coat as I entered the room. "Yes, it's mink, it's one hundred percent all mink, and it's all mine." She sounded almost like she was singing. She stood up and whirled around like the models do at the end of the runway. "Sam gave it to me for my birthday, and now he and Gary are going to the bakery to get me a cake. You'll have to come have some. This is a day I've always dreamed about, the day when I, Phyllis Grey, would have everything I ever wanted, a beautiful home, a baby, and a mink coat. Ain't it something how much I love this coat? It's the best."

Mrs. Rizzo ran to where I was standing and gave me a big, long, hot furry hug.

As Mrs. Rizzo and I unwound ourselves, my mother said, "That's great, Phyllis. I'm really happy for you."

The hint of Mother's envy was gone, and I stumbled to get the words out. "Me, too, Mrs. Rizzo. This is great. Happy Birthday."

In an earlier conversation about Mrs. Rizzo, when my mother wanted to caution me about not using words such as "ain't," she told me that Mrs. Rizzo had lived through a difficult past. She had been one of five children in a poor family. She'd never been a good student and had to take a year off during high school to work for the family. She'd worked as a waitress until Arnie Newton recognized what a beautiful girl she was and asked her to work for him at the Oldsmobile garage. She got the job of receptionist, where she could greet everyone who came in the door. Sometimes, on sale days, Arnie asked her to sit on the hood of one of the new Oldsmobiles in the showroom window to encourage male customers to come in and take a look.

Mother said that while Mrs. Rizzo was always grateful to Mr. Newton for giving her a job and for helping her to meet Sam when he came into the showroom on one of the days she was posing in the window, she missed not graduating from high school. As a result, when Sam asked her to marry him, she asked if she could quit her job and complete high school. When he said "yes," she said "yes" and declared him to be the man who could make all of her dreams come true.

My mother had told me that the reason Phyllis used crude words like "ain't" was because she had completed high school through a correspondence course. She hadn't had the advantage of going all the way through high school, reminding me I should show my gratitude by overcoming my urge to use the word "ain't." For the most part, Mother's admonition worked; however, on this day, Mother and I weren't thinking about the past, or lessons learned. Instead, we smiled with our fur-clad friend, enjoying whatever victory it was that she thought she had won.

That day, and the introduction of Mrs. Rizzo's mink coat, remains a vivid memory. An hour after I left the table and returned to the kitchen in my madras shorts, my mother and Mrs. Rizzo were still sitting in the kitchen having iced tea. Mrs. Rizzo remained in her mink, without sweating, until just before supper time. Before she left, she laughed and said, "You know I'll have to wear this coat everywhere, every day of my life to make it worth the extravagance. I just can't believe that little Phyllis Grey has a one hundred percent full-length mink coat."

In retrospect, I know now that the mink coat became a symbol for Mrs. Rizzo. It was something she had, something she would keep, and something that would indicate her own value to herself over time.

The Fifties and early Sixties were, after all, the age of fur, the time when wearing animals of any kind made women feel special. Diamonds had come, remained popular, and were forever; however, fur was for even more special times, the times in life that were simply over the top.

One year, my mother and father bought my grandmother a single strand of three mink, acknowledged as a mini stole, where the animals' bodies were kept intact, with heads, tails, and tiny eyes clearly visible. Each animal was attached, with each animal seeming to bite the tail of the next.

When my brother and I saw the three-pelt mini stole, we cried out in horror, asking out loud when someone would think of having a stole made out of the pelts of small dogs, perhaps of wiener dogs like our dog, Skipper.

"Oh, shush," my mother said. "This is real fur. Your grandmother deserves minks like these. They'll look just like a beautiful necklace on her pink suit."

My mother was angered by our response to my grandmother's extravagant gift. To remedy the situation, she asked Mrs. Rizzo to come over to reassure my grandmother. In no time at all, Mrs. Rizzo appeared, in her fur, as always, to tell my grandmother how good mink made a person feel. While my grandmother never looked comfortable in her stole of mink pelts, my mother, Mrs. Rizzo, and the other neighborhood women of the era "oohed" and "aahed" over my grandmother's minks every time they saw her wear her stole.

I grew older, entering a new era in which fur lost some of its luster. However, the lesson of that time was not entirely lost on me. I learned never to underestimate the power and self-esteem that can go along with extravagant gifts.

Years later, when Mrs. Rizzo attended my wedding, her marriage had ended with Sam's death. She sat in the third pew wearing her mink coat through the whole service. As she reached to hug me in the receiving line, I noticed that the seam of the coat had become unraveled under one arm. A slit of silk material peeked through, but Mrs. Rizzo seemed happy and confident. She made a champagne toast at the reception, thrusting her arm, covered by the unraveling mink sleeve high into the air. "Celebrate the good times!" she said. "Let's always remember these good times."

As Mrs. Rizzo aged, she faced financial ruin in her widowhood. Her beauty faded, her make-up became more severe, and lines began to show on her withering face. However, through it all, Mrs. Rizzo continued to wear her mink coat. She wore it to the Social Security office to collect Sam's widow benefits. She wore it to church as she prayed for better times. She wore it to the funeral of her only son, who died of AIDS. Through progressively bad times, the coat continued to comfort her with warm memories.

On the last day of her life, Phyllis Rizzo went to the mail box to get her mail, dressed in a flowered nightie, a light blue pair of Deerfoam flip-flops, and her mink coat. It was a cold day and a mixture of snow and ice covered the steps to her back door. As she returned from getting the mail, she fell as she approached the door and remained hidden behind the bushes that had become overgrown in front of her small back porch.

No one found her until morning, when one of the neighbor boys came to see if she wanted him to shovel the snow that had fallen during the night. Her body was stretched across the porch. In her left hand, she still held a copy of *People* magazine and a bill from the electric company. Her right hand looked as though it had been reaching for the doorknob. The whole porch scene was covered with patches of snow.

The ambulance driver said she looked "like sleeping beauty." He said he could still tell she'd been wearing red lipstick. And that she didn't look afraid or even frightened, but more like she'd been surprised.

The ambulance driver had visited our house to comfort my mother. He returned to our house to talk to her because he knew she'd become very upset when the body was discovered. Mother couldn't calm down because she felt responsible. She thought she should have seen Mrs. Rizzo through the window in time to save her.

"You couldn't have seen her," the driver said. I'm telling you all this because I think you should know it was probably just her time to go. The doctors all said she had a big stroke, and likely was dead before she fell. You don't need to feel guilty."

My mother cried as she gave me the news over the phone. "He was trying to make me feel better. I thanked him. It was very kind of him to think of me," she sobbed. "I'm going to miss Phyllis," she continued. "All these years, all the ups and downs, we started young and saw it all together. Now it's a different time. Phyllis was just going to get the mail. God, how she loved that coat."

Shortly after the funeral, Danny, Mrs. Rizzo's nephew, and his wife moved into her house. My mother said they were good kids and good neighbors. She said they'd humored her by cutting down the bushes in front of the porch, but then she didn't say much more about Mrs. Rizzo for a very long time.

Years later, when I was home for a visit, my mother stood at the kitchen window. She looked across the street at Rizzo's house and whispered, "I still miss her." Then she asked with a smile, "Do you remember the day she got the mink coat?" When I nodded, she laughed and whirled around as though she were modeling, "Ain't it somethin' how she loved that coat?"

Wouldn't You Really Rather Drive a Buick?

1963 Buick Riviera.

* ✷ *

I remember driving from our little town in Northern Ohio to my uncle's summer home on a small lake in Wisconsin. As we began our trip on I-80, the new Ohio Turnpike, I remember my father telling me that the highway was a gift from God, a place where any red-blooded American could find out why his Buick was better than a Ford, and where, occasionally, you could see funny-looking beetle-shaped cars from somewhere else entirely.

"Damn rat traps," my father called them. He could expound on what was wrong with them from Cleveland to Chicago. "They look like bugs, move like bugs, hopping up and down the highway; people who drive them look bug-eyed and suspicious."

"Why, we're blessed to live in the Midwest," he'd say, "where people are friendly and where we make the things that make this country great. We make cars, the best in the world, and even though we know that General Motors cars are better than Fords and way out of the league of Chrysler, it's good that everyone can have one of these dependable American-made models to put in their garage."

As we got closer to Chicago, he'd talk as he did, always non-stop, never dependent on having a listening audience, while my mother read a magazine and my brother and I were privileged to play "I spy" in the generous back seat of yet another new Buick. Sometimes, he interrupted himself long enough to point things out.

"Look there," he'd say, pointing to the smokestacks of the steel plants as the road skirted Gary, Indiana.

"Boy, Gary stinks," my brother answered, but my father always had a comeback.

"If Gary doesn't stink, it will be bad for all of us," he said, as he took a handkerchief from his pocket to blow his nose. As he blew loudly, my mother chimed in.

"For heaven's sake, Bob, keep it down. Do you want your children to blow like that when they're in a crowd? Everyone will think they have no manners at all."

"Ah, hell," my father replied. "Someday, I'll really show you what I can do if I really blow hard. Anyway, as I was saying, Gary stinks because it's making steel for the world. We need to be grateful for that smell even though it's not the best smell and even when it irritates our senses."

"Watch your language, Bob," my mother added.

We both laughed in the back seat, knowing that this could go on until we reached Wisconsin.

"I'm telling you, there would be no Buicks like this one, not even many of those little peanut cars if Gary didn't belch out that steel smoke. There are some things that these kids should know, like everything costs something, and we're the greatest country on Earth because we've always been willing to work hard to pay the price. We're not whiners like the French. We're not just blowhards like the Germans, either. We just work hard, get things done in a way that's fair and good for everyone. What's good for Gary is good for us, and what's good, especially for General Motors, forecasts the future of our whole world."

"Take a break, Bob," my mother said as she closed down the conversation. "We've got a long way to go."

"Well then, watch this, kids. I'll help you experience something that's powerful but a little more quiet. Pay attention to this horsepower."

We'd been playing tic-tac-toe on a little travel blackboard we'd brought along to play games in the car, but suddenly, we could feel the car accelerate. First, just a little, then, as we felt the car shift, the whole car quietly burst into rocket ride.

We looked out the window. Only a hint of smoke remained on the highway behind us. We were passing everything in sight—trucks, peanut cars, station wagons, vehicles of all kinds, including a Corvette.

"Bob," my mother said, and we sensed that a new conversation was beginning. "What are you doing? Have you lost your mind or are you just crazy? You'll get picked up, and what kind of example will that set anyway? Just slow down. Now, that's enough, Bob. I'm not kidding."

"Dena, I'm showing the kids how perfect and quiet this Buick can be. I'm in complete control. Now it's your turn to quiet down, observe, and enjoy the ride."

We passed at least four more cars, an ice cream truck, and four semi-trailer trucks.

"Well, look at this one kids; it's pulling double trailers. We wouldn't get to Wisconsin until tomorrow if we had to stay behind him in a peanut car."

We continued to look outside as the miles, signs, and endless vehicles disappeared in the rear view mirror.

"Really, Bob," my mother repeated. "I'm not kidding."

He laughed, tipped his head so he could see us in the mirror, and winked at us.

"Okay, Dena, but tell me now—aren't you really glad we drive a Buick?"

We arrived a few hours later at the lake house, where we could see our relatives running to greet us. As they helped unload our luggage, my uncle asked my father, "How do you like your Buick, Bob?"

"I just love it, Henry," my father replied. "You certainly couldn't get all this stuff in the trunk of any other car. Besides, Henry, you and I know that everyone in their right mind would rather have a Buick. A Buick looks rich, but not Cadillac rich, so it lets my customers know I've got good taste, but I still need their order. It's perfect, Henry, just perfect or damn near, damn near perfect.

The two men laughed and my dad punched Uncle Henry on the shoulder, then closed the lid of the trunk. As Henry started for the house, my father hesitated for a minute to look at his Buick. He smiled and shook his head. As he walked to catch up with my uncle, I could hear him mutter, under his breath, "Damn near perfect."

Coda

This story reminded me that things have changed radically in big areas of our country—in industry, opportunity, and even the use of certain words whose meaning has changed so much that my father would not use them. To him, winners were people who were inspired to do good things for everyone, and losers were not rotten apples just because they had less, or because they came from different backgrounds.

He warned us about Gary, and today there is no longer any stink from pulsing smoke stacks that used to send steel around the world. There also are no more assembly plants or parts manufacturers in the towns of northern Ohio. What's left is unemployment, For Sale signs, store closings, and families moving in with one another.

We lived in what is now a depressed county in our state, one where almost everyone had enough, where neighbors drove cars from General Motors, unless you were one of the few who worked at the Ford plant. Occasionally, someone bought a Chrysler, but no one drove "foreign cars," which meant, without mention, that you should not drive anything "foreign" either.

I take what hope I can from what my father said as he blazed along I-80 in his brand-new Buick, blissfully unaware of what was to come. "Remember," he said, "Americans don't whine, they buck up." Today, I hope we all can believe that, especially in the town I came from. I hope we can rise again, like good Americans, doing what's right and fair for everyone.

Thankfully, Buick was allowed to survive. That would have been a bit of consolation for my father. He had said more than once, if he ever came back to this life, he'd be happy to return as a Buick. For today at least, Dad still has another chance.

Afterword

Art of a new generation.

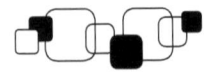

In the sixth grade, my grandson wrote the following response to a class writing prompt "Where do you come from?". In meeting this assignment, he created an end to my stories and a wonderful beginning for family stories that are yet to come.

Where I Come From
I am from the old painting on the kitchen wall, the waiter and his tray.
From Otter Pops and Ham and Cheddar Hot Pockets® on lazy afternoons
I am from the dark gray walls and the cold brown of the new wooden floor, to the grass, soft as I tread by, and the towering cottonwood, a behemoth behind the glass.
I am from the dying maple as it sheds its deep greens for pale yellows, as the years drag on.

I am from the family dinners, a sea of gold and brown hair.
I am from the slow crackle as heat dances across my face, making a ballet on the dark sky,
From the long weeks spilling into not long enough weekends.
I am from the Sundays full of football, family and fun.

I'm from cold Boston winters to the blazing Texas summers, From sweet, savory lemonade and freshly grilled hamburgers, hold the tomatoes.

I am from the fear of the crowds smiling face, the long nights gazing at diamonds in the sky.

I am from the bright white hair, playing card games for hours, the one that always cheats. The loveable evenings full of laughter, joy, and wonderful moments.

I'm from these halls lined with the faces and places of memories passed, the years before I came at last, providing new lines to the story these walls show, adding to the times before my story was told.

—Ryan Armour, age 11

With Gratitude

In our new home.

To all those who helped me live these stories, and for all of those who helped me tell them.

Special thanks to everyone in our writing group "The Writing Lab": Ronnie, Kathy, Randy, Felicia, Beth, Nancy, Doug, Norma, and, of course, my husband Roger. Thanks also to my friend Veronica Patterson, always a cheerleader, who edited and helped me shape this book. Also, many thanks to my friend Emily Rogers Ramos who generously agreed to be my reader.
She made great suggestions and provided great support for this endeavor.

Also, with great appreciation to Robin Shukle and Liz Mrofka at What If? Publishing for putting this book together with great skill and imagination.

Years of thanks to my fabulous coffee friends who have listened to way too many stories, too many times, and continue to encourage me anyway.

Finally, thanks to an incredible, always interesting family. Roger knows the cast of these stories so well that he sometimes tells them as his own. Daughter Kelly and husband Rob provided the gift of a book of family questions that created the idea for this book. Our younger grandson Ryan allowed me to use his wonderful artwork and poetry to create what I hope is the beginning of stories to follow. My mathematically talented older grandson, Matt faithfully continues to listen to my questionable ramblings, providing lots of laughter in the process. He allows me to be as silly as I want to be as an ardent and kind supporter.

From a distance, credit also goes to those who share the Columbi gene, either by birth or by choice. Here's to brother Tim, my sister, sister-in-law Penny, their Son Ben, and daughter Alex and husband Dave, and to the newest Columbi grandson Jack! Their genes make them all serious partners in sharing the family history.

It was a great ride.

Made in the USA
San Bernardino, CA
19 March 2019